MOONLIGHT AND KISSES

"Do you know what I'd like?" Mark asked, his eyes filled with desire.

"What?" Allegra said breathlessly.

"I would like to make very slow, delicious love to you. All night long." His eyes never left hers, and she felt her heart jump. She trembled as Mark tenderly ran his hands through her thick, wavy hair, lifting it sensuously and letting it drop again to her shoulders. His face in the moonlight was mesmerizing, his tawny eyes smoldered with intensity. "Tell me you want me," he said. "Tell me."

"I do," she whispered, as a deep fevered well of passion rose within her. "I do want you. . . ."

DIANA MORGAN is a pseudonym for a husband-and-wife writing team. They enjoy opera, feasting, studying the Real Estate section of *The New York Times*, and figuring out what will happen next on *Hill Street Blues*. They met at a phone booth at Columbia University, and have been together romantically and professionally ever since. Read their previous Rapture Romances: *Ocean Fires, Lady In Flight, Amber Dreams, Emerald Dreams*, and *Crystal Dreams*.

Dear Reader:

We at Rapture Romance hope you will continue to enjoy our four books each month as much as we enjoy bringing them to you. Our commitment remains strong to giving you only the best, by well-known favorite authors and exciting new writers.

We've used the comments and opinions we've heard from *you*, the reader, to make our selections, so please keep writing to us. Your letters have already helped us bring you better books—the kind you want—and we appreciate and depend on them. Of course, we are always happy to forward mail to our authors—writers need to hear from their fans!

Happy reading!

The Editors
Rapture Romance
New American Library
1633 Broadway
New York, NY 10019

HIDDEN FIRES

by

Diana Morgan

RAPTURE ROMANCE

NEW AMERICAN LIBRARY

NAL BOOKS ARE AVAILABLE AT QUANTITY DISCOUNTS
WHEN USED TO PROMOTE PRODUCTS OR SERVICES.
FOR INFORMATION PLEASE WRITE TO PREMIUM MARKETING DIVISION,
NEW AMERICAN LIBRARY, 1633 BROADWAY,
NEW YORK, NEW YORK 10019.

SIGNET, SIGNET CLASSIC, MENTOR, PLUME, MERIDIAN AND NAL BOOKS
are published by New American Library,
1633 Broadway, New York, New York 10019

First Printing, December, 1984

1 2 3 4 5 6 7 8 9

PRINTED IN THE UNITED STATES OF AMERICA

To K.T., A.T.
&
the Mangia Society

Chapter One

The Gotham Men's Club was located in the heart of Manhattan, and it was legendary that no woman had ever penetrated its interior. The club remained a stalwart haven for local businessmen, retaining its turn-of-the-century aura through potted palms, deep burgundy velvets, dark brown leather sofas, and elegant antique spittoons. Women weren't exactly prohibited, but no woman had ever tried to break the barrier and join. Perhaps women were intimidated by the legend and preferred not to make waves, or perhaps it was simply that they weren't interested in an island of masculinity that had long since lost its luster. Whatever the reason, the club remained a masculine domain year after year—until the day Allegra Russo decided to break tradition.

Mark Trackman sat in his usual corner of the lounge when Allegra sauntered in, and he was the only man there who did not notice her entrance.

Allegra's long, sleek legs paraded through the lobby as her high heels clicked on the parquet floor. She stopped abruptly in front of Mark Trackman, who was lounging casually in an overstuffed armchair, directly underneath a glassy-eyed moose head that was mounted on the wall. He remained silent, as did the other, rather stuffy-looking gentlemen in the lounge, as if she were a gnat to be annoyingly shooed away. Only one kindly gray-haired man in the corner seemed to take any interest in her. Leaning forward on his brass-topped cane to get a better look at her, the elderly man smiled slowly.

Allegra looked accusingly at the insolent figure in the armchair. "Okay, Trackman!" she huffed. "This time you've gone too far."

The latest edition of *Trailblazer*, the magazine which Trackman published, lowered inch by inch, revealing a strong bronzed face. An eyebrow arched as he took in the sight of the breathless young woman in front of him.

"Would you mind explaining yourself?" she demanded, taking a stubborn stance. He let out a bemused sigh, which aggravated Allegra even more. "You really have a lot of nerve," she continued, refusing to let him deflate her anger. "Do you know that? Do you?"

Mark Trackman contemplated her. The wizened old man in the corner was polishing his spectacles for a closer look at the spectacle, but Trackman's interest in Allegra obviously stemmed from a purely masculine source. His elegant body languidly filled the chair, which seemed to be merely a prop set there to display his rakish form. He had blond hair and patrician features, but his eyes were a devilish golden brown, sparkling with impatient intelligence and wit. He was the only man there not wearing a suit, but his sturdy khaki trousers, work shirt, and worn hiking boots were not at all out of place, for they matched the appearance of the musty paintings on the walls, depicting turn-of-the-century hunters posed rigidly in front of trapped prey, rifles and safari hats in tow. If nothing else, his clothes were decidedly masculine, enforcing the stubborn refusal of the Gotham Men's Club to make the leap into the twentieth century. His costume was certainly in character for the publisher of *Trailblazer* magazine, who was the walking image of all that his male-oriented periodical represented.

Allegra inhaled sharply as he scrutinized her. Perhaps she should have worn something more conservative, she thought, but she hadn't come here to impress anyone. Besides, she didn't own anything that could be called conservative. Her rosy floral-printed halter dress with its flared skirt and the high-heeled sandals on her feet had seemed to her a fitting enough presentation for the elusive Mr. Trackman. Her brown eyes glowed in her lively, oval face, their sparkle heightened by the unruly mass of dark curls that cascaded over her ears and down to her shoulders. Gold hoop earrings dangled on either side of her face, and a bandanalike scarf was tied gypsy-style around her head. Allegra noticed Mark Trackman's nose twitch slightly as the scent of her musky perfume floated by his nostrils.

"Miss Russo," he said slowly, enunciating his words with detached deliberation. "Just what exactly are you doing here? Surely you must be aware . . ." He gestured delicately, as if the unspoken code of the club was too sacred to utter aloud.

"Oh, can it, Trackman," she said so abruptly that he laughed and let his hand drop. "I'm not interested in some moldy old code that no one cares about anymore."

His eyes traveled briefly around the room. "No one? I think these gentlemen care. They care a great deal. Do you really have the temerity to thumb your nose at a century worth of venerable tradition?" His voice resounded, as if he were reciting a passage from Shakespeare. Allegra nodded emphatically, her eyes flashing and the earrings bobbing up and down. "Surely you're not that insensitive," he finished, undaunted.

"Look," she said, trying a new tack. "I tried to call you several times, but you never answered my messages—as usual. So I took the chance of finding you here. Apparently it worked."

He nodded, clearly amused. "How very clever of you. Obviously, however, you failed to interpret my silence. I'm afraid we're not interested in your proposal, Miss Russo. The answer is no."

"But . . ."

"Please. Let's not create a scene."

She stood her ground, her determination evident in the firm lines of her stance. "Mr. Trackman, I have been renting the office next door to this club for two years and for two years you've ignored me. You never fix things, you never answer calls. All you do is collect the rent."

"If you're not happy here, we'll be happy to cancel your lease," he said hopefully.

"I would be perfectly happy if you would simply allow me to rent the vacant space in this building which adjoins my office next door."

"I'm afraid you already know that's quite impossible."

"But *why*?" she demanded. "Because I'm a woman?"

"Please, Miss Russo." He dismissed her with a weary toss of his head. "Don't start reciting feminist jargon to me. The answer will still be no. The building next door is one thing, but *this* building is the home of the Gotham Men's Club. Women are not allowed."

"That has nothing to do with it," she said hotly. "It's against the law to discriminate against potential tenants. I came here with a perfectly good offer, and you don't even want to hear it."

"No, I don't. Why waste time?"

Her foot tapped on the worn carpet as she eyed his arrogant face. "Your little club is in trouble, Mr. Trackman. You're taking in boarders, just like a little old lady who needs the extra income. You need a tenant, and I'm ready to sign the lease. You can't afford to be choosy, you know."

"Who's denying it?" He shrugged. "But this is still a private concern, and we still have rules to uphold."

"But I can't believe you'd be so . . . so petty, so disgustingly . . ."

"Male chauvinist?" he filled in for her. "Ah, yes. It looks like we're going to be subjected to feminist jargon after all. I have nothing against women, Miss Russo. Or should I say 'Ms.'?"

"You should."

"Very well. But we are entitled to our privacy. And right now, you are invading it."

"I'm not invading anything. I'm making you a perfectly reasonable business offer."

"Which I am turning down," he said with mock patience. "You already know the reasons."

"Well, I'd like to hear them all the same," she said stubbornly. "For the record."

His perfectly carved mouth settled into a tight little line. "The Gotham Men's Club exists so that *men* can assemble peaceably and privately. It is a haven from the outside world where *men* can relax, enjoy the company of their peers, and rely on the discretion of the establishment to protect them from undue concerns while they are here. Is that so difficult to understand?"

"Not at all," she said smoothly. "It sounds lovely. In fact, it sounds like something I'd like to join."

"Forget it."

"Why?" she demanded. "Give me one logical reason. Maybe I'd like the same discretion, the same protection, the same mingling with peers, or whatever you called it. Am I not entitled to that, just as you are?"

"Certainly," he said in a perfectly composed voice. "But not here."

"You think women aren't good enough to join your precious club?"

"It has nothing to do with that."

"Well, I'd like to know just what it does have to do with."

He sighed elaborately. "There are times, *Ms.* Russo, when men simply want to be among themselves, away from the distractions of women."

"Distractions?" Her voice was incredulous. "You make us sound like seductive sirens who think of nothing but charming the pants off you men." She stopped short at her unintentional double entendre, and he managed only partially to stifle a grin.

"Aptly put, Ms. Russo."

She threw back her head in a gesture of frustration. "Why is it that men always assume women are out to ensnare them? I assure you, that is the furthest thing from my mind. I think the real issue here is that you have some kind of adolescent hang-up that prevents you from seeing women as regular human beings."

She calmed down slightly, happy with that speech, but Mark was totally unimpressed. "And you keep missing the point," he said. "Men have every right to be alone with members of their own sex if they want to. Women do it all the time, under the banner of feminism. Why aren't we entitled to the same privilege?"

Allegra floundered, caught off guard by his logic. She hadn't expected her own arguments thrown back in her face. How had this conversation become so stinging, anyway? All she wanted was to rent the upstairs space to accommodate her expanding business. He was turning the issue into a crisis of national proportions.

"Look," she said, trying to sound reasonable. "All I want is that space upstairs. It won't interfere with your privacy, or with mine."

"Why do you need it so badly?" he asked suspiciously.

"My business is expanding," she answered eagerly, thinking that he was opening up at last.

"Your business? I never did understand that club of yours." He was using the tone of a Scotland Yard investigator, but Allegra played along, hoping to find a chink in the fortress. "The Mangia Society," she explained patiently, "is a club dedicated to the enjoyment and celebration of great food. I put out a newsletter and offer mail order items at a discount. It's been doing very well, and I need space in which to hold parties and banquets. If you could just . . ."

He raised an eyebrow and looked her up and down with severe doubt. "It all sounds decidedly hedonistic to me," he remarked darkly. "A bunch of revelers constantly feasting in this building? It's hardly what we had in mind."

"Don't be ridiculous," she snapped, trying to control her temper. "If a gourmet banquet is your idea of a Roman orgy, then you really do have a problem."

"My only problem at the moment," he said calmly, "is how to gracefully get you out of this building without creating further mishap."

"I had no idea you'd be so unreasonable about this," she huffed, ignoring his last statement. She noticed the elderly gentleman in the corner was listening to the argument with growing amusement, and his interest emboldened her even more. She strolled right up to Trackman's chair, her wide skirt brushing carelessly against his knee.

"Oh, no," he lamented dryly. "Please don't try some sort of mindless flirtation. I really can't stomach that sort of thing."

"You should be so lucky," she said with a smirk. She looked down at his rugged clothing and was impressed with the impeccable look despite its sturdy intent. There was something undeniably dashing about this man, and she didn't really want to fight him. Perhaps he was only testing her, waiting to see if he could get her dander up.

"I was just wondering," she said coolly, "what your current membership is. I get the impression it could use a boost."

"The number of members is not important," he said stonily. "What counts is that they are all men."

She restrained her annoyance once again. "Why don't you all take a vote on opening up the membership to women? You just might be surprised."

"Don't be ridiculous. Our members are all over the age of sixty-five—with one obvious exception. They're too old to change. The only reason I'm a member is because my father was, and I believe in keeping up a tradition. Not that I don't enjoy it," he added hastily. "I appreciate the privacy and the service. At least I did until today, when you interrupted my very pleasant afternoon."

Allegra looked around doubtfully. "Privacy? I'll say. This place reminds me of a museum. Possibly a morgue." She traced a finger along the wooden ridge at the top of his chair and lifted it to show him the dust. "Can't you even afford a maid? A male maid, of course."

He shrugged. "Typical remark of a fussy female. It so happens that this club was started by contemporaries of Teddy Roosevelt. They were all rugged individualists, outdoorsmen who didn't bother themselves about a speck of dust here and there." His eyes took on a distant glaze. "We used to have over five hundred members."

Allegra was impressed in spite of herself. "Really? This must have been quite a place at one time. Uh . . . how many do you have now?"

"Ninety-three," he said flatly.

"Ninety-three?" She looked around again, restraining a smile. "What happened to the rest? They all resigned? Their memberships expired?"

"No. Their memberships didn't expire. They did."

There was a pause as this remark sank in.

"I see. Well, what are you going to do when all of the members have . . . expired?"

He stood up suddenly, his lanky form drawing itself to its full height with fluid grace. The thought that Mark Trackman was probably a terrific dancer crossed Allegra's mind, but she immediately dismissed it as inappropriately absurd. This mountain-climbing, trailblazing macho man was hardly the type to be waltzing around a dance floor. "That, my dear lady, is none of your business," he announced with considerable dignity. Allegra bristled, disconcerted by the now obvious difference in their heights. He towered head and shoulders over her, making her feel suddenly and uncomfortably like a self-righteous midget challenging an Adonis. The only way she could confront him was to crane her neck and stare directly up at him. It was like looking up at a statue.

"Please," she said uncomfortably. "Can't we discuss this reasonably?" It was a desperate statement. She already knew she had lost. Why did she want to stand there jousting with him? Was it because she actually enjoyed talking to him?

Her mind darted back fleetingly over the two years

that she had been renting her office from Mark Track-man. He had not been a model landlord. He had rarely returned her calls, and when she did talk to him, the conversations tended to be as baffling and impossible as this one had been. Yet oddly enough, they had found a hesitant sort of rapport with each other. There was a rhythm and a subtle wit to their arguments that had a perverse appeal. She had grown used to it and wondered if he felt it too. For no reason at all, she would find herself smiling at odd moments at one of the more outrageous things he had said to her, though there was no rhyme or reason for such behavior. They had nothing in common; their values were worlds apart. But for some crazy reason she actually enjoyed his stubborn logic, if only because it matched hers. They were always two brick walls, always facing off.

Mark looked down at her quizzically with a bemused expression. His usual defiance was temporarily gone, and Allegra took heart. "We do seem to be going around in circles, don't we?" she said at last.

He smiled suddenly, a radiant smile that lit up his whole face. "We finally agree on something." He nodded, making her laugh.

"I can think of one other thing we could agree on," she said slyly.

"What's that?"

"I've been a pretty good tenant, haven't I?" He started to interrupt, and she held up a hand. "I know, I know, I'm always complaining about things breaking down, but it is your job to fix them. I always pay the rent on time, don't I?"

He was obliged to nod. "We're not exactly charging you an arm and a leg," he couldn't resist pointing out.

"Well, you shouldn't, considering the service," she

bristled. "It's not easy trying to cook in there, you know. I might do better if I was a midget."

He nodded again, this time with a gleeful twinkle in his eye. "I have to admit, there have been some tantalizing smells coming out of that room from time to time. Last week it smelled like cinnamon. It was perfectly heavenly."

Allegra brightened, pleased that he had noticed. "That's right. I was baking chocolate cinnamon tortes."

His face changed with sudden interest, as if he couldn't help betraying the fact that her pursuits were of a definite universal appeal. "Sounds delicious," he said finally, shifting almost imperceptibly.

Yet the tiny movement was enough to tell Allegra that she had gotten to him at last. Even the unmovable Mark Trackman could be swayed at the mention of mouthwatering food. She suppressed a smile before saying, "Perhaps you'd like to come to a Mangia Society gathering some time. Then you could see for yourself just what this hedonistic club is all about."

She watched as his face became a mask once again. "Is this a social invitation?" he asked archly.

She pondered. "Uh—well, not exactly. I just thought you might want to . . ." The sentence was left unfinished, and she knew she had gone too far. Trackman was not like other men; he wasn't like anyone she had ever known. She had never been able to figure him out, and her annoyance rose again even as she acknowledged that their strange, irresistible rapport had been shiningly present for several delicious moments. "Oh, never mind," she said. "It was a bad idea."

"Not necessarily," he said calmly, making her swallow in surprise. "But it won't have any effect on my decision

about what goes on in this building. You are confusing
the issues. As usual," he added sardonically.

Her eyes flashed with their customary brilliance. It
was back to business as usual. She took a step backward,
lessening the dramatic effect of the difference in their
heights. She wished he would sit down again but sensed
that he remained towering over her just to unnerve her. It
hardly seemed fair that he could hold himself with casual
masculine confidence while it was all she could do to keep
herself from staring at his long, hard form with frank
interest.

"I think I'll be leaving now," she mumbled, focusing
on the chair behind him. There was no point in
continuing this discussion any longer because she knew it
would come up again as it always did.

"Well, don't let me keep you," he said at once. "You
aren't supposed to be in here in the first place, you
know."

Allegra pressed her lips together and hid the rushing
hurt that suddenly assailed her. She had no idea why this
remark, after all their banter, should bother her, but it
did. It was as if he really didn't want her there, not only
because of the antiquated club rules, but because he simply didn't like her. Perhaps he didn't secretly enjoy their
fiery little debates as she did. Allegra felt she was making
a big mistake: he couldn't possibly care *that* much about
the club's rules because no one else in the dusty room
did. After her initial impression, most of the men had
returned to their newspapers. Only the one sprightly old
man in the corner still watched her with amused interest.

She searched her mind for a parting shot. "That wasn't
necessary," she said coldly. "You don't have to add rude-
ness to your other dubious qualifications."

A look of apology darted across his face, but he

repressed it upon noticing Allegra's icy stare. "I wasn't being rude," he said. "I was merely pointing out the obvious. You're still here, and you aren't supposed to be. Perhaps—perhaps we can continue this discussion at a more appropriate time."

A kindly voice interrupted them. "May I help you, my dear?" Allegra stepped back and blinked as the elderly gentleman from the corner approached them. He was wearing a conservative three-piece suit with an old-fashioned watch chain, and his lined face did not belie his still-adventurous spirit. Despite his use of an elegant, brass-topped cane, he walked with sprightly energy.

"She was just leaving, Wendell," Mark said pointedly. "I'm sorry you had to be disturbed. It's a shame. After all these years . . ."

"Nonsense," the older man said brusquely. He turned to Allegra, his eyes twinkling. "It's my pleasure to meet you, young lady. You're like a breath of fresh air in this old place." Allegra was surprised, but she managed to send Mark Trackman a cool, triumphant glance. "I was about to leave myself," Wendell continued. He extended his arm in a courtly gesture. "Allow me."

Allegra took his arm with crushing poise, and the two of them sailed out of the room without a backward glance. Mark Trackman was left to stew in his own juices.

"Is he for real?" Allegra asked, when they were out of the musty confines of the club and back on the busy, sun-lit street.

Wendell smiled. "It all depends on what you mean. Thanks to Mark and his shrewd business acumen, the club has managed to stay afloat much longer than any of us old-timers thought possible."

"Why, how old is he?" she asked curiously.

"Oh, thirty-seven or thirty-eight, I suppose. Compared to the rest of us, he's a youngster."

"Well, he's a terrible landlord," she said disapprovingly. "I didn't have any heat for two weeks this winter. His only response was to tell me to dress warmly!"

"I know." Wendell nodded ruefully. "We had the same problem, you know. I'm afraid that old boiler in the basement is on its last legs. And when it goes, so does the Gothem Men's Club."

Allegra had respect for his sense of history, but she was still too riled by Mark's attitude to be overly sympathetic. "Just how does Trackman fit into all this, anyway?" she asked. "Doesn't he ever hang out with people his own age?"

"His great-grandfather was one of the club's founding members," Wendell said with a nostalgic sigh. He pointed to the side of the building, where a plaque quietly proclaimed the club's origins. Allegra stared at it with frank interest. She had been renting space for two years, but she had never noticed the plaque before.

GOTHAM MEN'S CLUB
"EXPLORATION IS OUR DESTINY"
April 12, 1887

FOUNDING MEMBERS
HORACE LIONEL EVERT
STERLING CARLISLE
JAMES PINCKNEY III
CALVIN JOHN TRACKMAN

Allegra's sharp brown eyes softened as she read the inscription. She couldn't resent the air of romanticism that lingered in the building. Yet it represented an era that was long gone, and Mark Trackman, the heir to the legend, steadfastly refused to face facts. "It's a shame," she said quietly. "But the club isn't going to last much longer, is it?"

"No, my dear, it's not," Wendell answered matter-of-factly. "And we will let it go in peace when the time comes. But until then, pride and tradition keep our chins up."

"I still think you're wrong," she said with quiet spirit, and he regarded her with admiration. "This club could have a whole new lease on life if you would just open your minds as well as the doors."

He chuckled. "Well, you could be right about that. But there's no sense in talking to an old-timer like me. Talk to young Trackman in there. He's the future here, not me."

She gazed doubtfully toward the heavy oak door with its lion's-head brass knobs. "But he's impossible. I might as well be talking to a wall."

"He's not so bad. He's just a confirmed old bachelor, that's all." He tipped his hat to her in a traditional gesture of politeness, and she nodded back, compelled to respond courteously. Oddly enough, she rather liked the time-honored motions. She watched as he moved off down the street, an erect, still-elegant figure with his own private sense of dignity.

She contemplated his words as she stood alone in front of the building. She had never dealt with a "confirmed old bachelor" before and it was news to her that there were such oddities left in the world. Mark Trackman was definitely the quintessential bachelor. And she had to admit that he was just about the most eligible bachelor she had ever met.

Chapter Two

❧

"He's a pighead!" Allegra exclaimed to her two friends over lunch the next day at her favorite restaurant. "A bona-fide male chauvinist pighead from the nineteenth century. Oh, how I wish you two had been there to see him! He's like something out of one of those old safari movies where the big, strong hero beats up a gorilla. Ugh!"

"Take it easy, Allegra." Sabrina Melendey reached over and gently touched her friend's arm. "He obviously had quite an effect on you."

"I'll say."

Sabrina looked at her friend candidly, through the eyes of an artist. She was accustomed to studying people's faces and moods, often shunning the obvious or the conventional, and at the moment, Allegra's flushed face was giving away more than Allegra knew. Sabrina looked as if she wanted to say more, but the waiter arrived with the bottle of wine they had ordered, uncorked it, and ceremoniously poured a sample into Allegra's glass. She seized the glass and took a quick swallow, assuming that the Saint Julien she had chosen would be satisfactory. It wasn't.

She choked and put the glass down, sloshing the liquid over onto the white tablecloth.

"Something is wrong, mademoiselle?" the waiter asked anxiously.

She nodded and took a gulp of water. "It's turned." She gestured toward the glass. "Try it, you'll see."

After a moment's hesitation, he did as she suggested, and his face immediately soured. "My apologies, mademoiselle," he said at once. "I will bring you another bottle." He glided off, leaving the three friends alone.

Veronica Quincy, the third companion, looked at Allegra in admiration. "You really know your stuff," she said, tossing her sleek black hair behind her.

"Never mind that," Sabrina broke in impatiently. "I want to hear more about this hunk you met yesterday." Her impish green eyes crinkled in fun in her delicate face.

"Hunk!" Allegra repeated in protest. "Give me a break. He's anything but."

"Uh-huh," Sabrina said, thoroughly unconvinced. "That guy's got you, Russo. I can tell."

"Oh, stop trying to make something out of nothing. You're an incurable matchmaker, Sabrina."

"I don't know." Veronica laughed. "I think Sabrina is right on target this time."

Allegra shook her head at the two of them. "Now don't you two get any of those crazy ideas of yours. I still haven't forgotten the disastrous blind date ten years ago that you rigged up for me during Homecoming Weekend."

They all laughed in remembrance. And after all these years, they hadn't really changed. The three had been inseparable in their college days, and together they had formed the beginnings of the Mangia Society. Originally an informal club with a loose membership, it was now a nation-wide organization under Allegra's expert direction.

"Well, he sounds like an interesting specimen," Sabrina insisted. "Sounds like someone we should check out."

"Now wait a minute," Allegra said, trying to sound stern. "I don't need a pair of den mothers, thank you very much."

Sabrina's eyes twinkled again with perception. "Methinks the lady is protesting too much. Don't you think so, Veronica?"

Allegra was spared the answer by the arrival of the waiter, who brought a new bottle of wine. "This is on the house," he informed them. "And may I suggest the cold trout mousse as an appetizer? Michel knows you are here and asked me to have you sample it."

"Thank you." Allegra beamed. "And please tell him I want the recipe if I like it."

He wagged a friendly finger at her. "Ah, that I cannot promise, mademoiselle." He poured her a glass of wine, and this time it was a success. Allegra sipped and nodded enthusiastically, and he filled the other glasses with skillful ease.

"That's the problem with the Mangia Society," Allegra complained when he had gone. "Half the great chefs in New York are members, but none of them are willing to share their recipes. All they want to do is steal everyone else's."

"Including yours," Veronica pointed out. "You shouldn't be so quick to publish them in the newsletter. Michel is only trying to protect the secrets that make him what he is."

Sabrina was sipping her wine with an intent expression. "So what does he do?" she asked after a short pause.

"His specialty is fish. He does it with a special kind of poacher that—"

"Not Michel." Sabrina giggled. "I meant this safari character."

Allegra sighed wearily. "You're not going to give up, are you?" Sabrina shook her head emphatically. "Okay. Think of him like this. He's an adventurer, all right, but not like your husband."

"Colin?" Sabrina laughed. "He hasn't been out of his office in over a year."

"Well, this guy has been. From the way he sounds, he's probably never at home. He's like a peacock parading his feathers. And he's so damn smug about it too!" She buried her face in her wineglass, and her two friends exchanged glances.

"I like him already," Sabrina said calmly, making Allegra choke on her wine. "Colin would probably love to meet him. I'm sure they'll have something in common."

"I doubt that," Allegra snapped. "Does Colin hunt? Does he go after innocent animals with vicious weapons?"

"No," Sabrina admitted. "He doesn't believe in interfering with nature. He observes it. He's a paleontologist, not a killer."

"Well, this character is disturbing more than just my nature," Allegra continued. "Colin studies ancient bones that he digs up, but Trackman is the one who puts them there."

"It sounds like Dan might like him," Veronica said brightly. "My husband gets along with just about all types."

"Dan would want to punch him out," Allegra said flatly. "He's so arrogant and assured, as if everything around him is too mundane to bother about. He's the kind of guy who would refer to climbing Mount Everest in the dead of winter as a day hike." Allegra laughed at her own joke, but her friends merely smiled knowingly. "Will you two please cut it out?" she pleaded.

"I didn't say a thing," Sabrina said innocently.

The waiter returned to take their orders, and Allegra breathed a sigh of relief. "We'll try that trout mousse," she said. He wrote the order down on his pad. "But only if I can have the recipe." He smiled and shook his head with a Gallic shrug. "I will try, Mademoiselle Russo. But I do not think so."

"Well, tell him I'll—" She paused, and a mischievous smile lit up her face. "Never mind. I'll tell him myself." She got up and walked briskly toward the kitchen before anyone could stop her, marching through the double doors with a determined expression. François, the assistant chef, looked up in alarm when he saw her, but Michel, the proprietor, merely smiled. They were standing together at a huge stove, peering into the contents of a small saucepan that held a sauce. Behind them, half a dozen assistants were busily chopping on the butcher block island in the center of the spotless kitchen, and three more were laboring at another enormous stove on the other wall.

"It's no use!" Michel called out merrily as she approached. "You may as well give up. I will never divulge my secret formula!"

She looked instinctively at the bevy of assistants, who wore nervous, tight-lipped expressions. "They are sworn to secrecy." He chuckled. Michel left his place at the stove and, taking her firmly by the arm, escorted her out of the kitchen and back to her table where her friends waited in amused anticipation. He held her chair for her until she was seated. Then he spoke with a broad smile. "My dear Allegra," he said authoritatively. "What you need is a man to cook for. It would keep you away from your club and in the kitchen, where you rightfully belong."

Allegra bristled, her dark eyes shooting sparks at him. "Another male chauvinist," she said resentfully.

"*Au contraire.* It was a compliment. Very few people belong in the kitchen—male or female. You are one of them." He tipped his tall chef's hat with elaborate deference and strolled off with an amused look on his ruddy face.

"Do you believe him?" Allegra asked, somewhat embarrassed.

"You're really striking out with men these days," Veronica observed candidly.

"I think he sounds dynamic," Sabrina said cheerfully. They both looked at her. "I'm talking about Mark Trackman," she said, as if they should have known. "Trackman . . . even his name makes him sound like an adventurer. And he's the editor of *Trailblazer* magazine? Hmmm. So we know he's not illiterate. Colin reads that magazine once in a while. In fact, he wrote an article for it once. Something about Eskimos and how they hunt for seals through the ice."

"Sounds about right." Allegra nodded grimly. "I think I saw a polar bear's head mounted on the wall of that club. I wouldn't be surprised if Trackman flew up to the Arctic, booked himself a room in the local igloo, and tried his luck at massacring innocent seals."

This time they all laughed, and the waiter returned with their appetizers.

"I have a great idea," Veronica said suddenly, tapping the waiter on the sleeve of his white jacket. "May we have a phone, please?"

"Certainly, mademoiselle."

Allegra looked up apprehensively, but Veronica put up a hand to calm her. "Don't worry. I know what I'm doing."

Sabrina giggled delightedly as a cordless phone was brought. Veronica pulled out the antenna, dialed Information, and jotted the number of the Gotham Men's Club on her napkin.

"What are you doing?" Allegra demanded, but Veronica waved the protest away. She punched the buttons quickly and waited as the phone rang on the other end.

"Mark Trackman, please," she said after a pause. She put her hand over the receiver. "They have a man answering," she whispered conspiratorially. "They sure stick to their guns." She giggled at her own pun, but straightened up with a sober look. "I think he's coming."

"Veronica," Allegra warned. "You'd better not . . ."

"Let me," Sabrina broke in quickly. "Quick, give me the phone, I know exactly what to do."

Before Allegra could interfere, Sabrina wrested the phone away from Veronica, her eyes sparkling. She waited breathlessly for a moment, and then she sat up suddenly. "Uh, yes, Mr. Trackman? My name is Sabrina Melendey. Perhaps you remember my husband, Colin Forrester?" There was a pause. "Yes, that's right," she continued. "The polar bear story." She winked at Veronica, trying to hold back her laughter. "Yes, well, I'm sure he would. As a matter of fact, we're giving a party tomorrow night down at my loft in SoHo, and we'd be delighted if you could come. We were hoping that you could give a little talk. . . . On what? . . . Oh! Uh, well, how about wilderness survival techniques?" There was another pause, during which she looked somewhat frazzled. "What kind of wilderness?" she said weakly. "Oh, I don't know." She looked at her friends helplessly. "Just any wilderness will do. Just pick a . . . a really good one. Any one you like." Veronica was laughing into her cupped hands, and Allegra was scowling darkly. Sabrina put a hand over the receiver and hissed, "He's laughing. Be quiet!" She listened again for a moment, blanching slightly at what she was hearing. "Oh, well you'd have to talk to him about that," she said. "But I think he might be interested. He was talking just the other day about some kind of club to go to after work." Allegra sat up, vastly amused by this, chortling behind her wineglass. "We'll see you tomorrow evening, then," Sabrina was saying. "Yes, eight o'clock will be fine." She gave him the address and hung up with a satisfied grin. "There," she said. "Mission accomplished."

"He wants Colin to join that club?" Allegra asked with a smirk.

"Well, yes." Sabrina squirmed. "I was just humoring him, of course. But that's not the point." She brightened and regarded her friends with an impish smile. "He's coming. And we'll all get to have a good look at him."

"Lucky us," Allegra mumbled.

"Especially you," Sabrina persisted. "It will give you a chance to get to know him better."

Veronica laughed and lifted her glass. "A toast!" she cried gaily. "To rugged individualism!"

"To macho men!" Sabrina added, getting right into the proper spirit. "To Mark Trackman, the last of his breed."

Allegra lifted her glass reluctantly but then smiled. "That's right," she said dryly. "The last of a dying breed. Genuine dodos." They all broke into raucous laughter and clinked their glasses together.

I'll tell you this, buddy. Hunting caribou in Alaska's tun-

*dra is no place for the lighthearted. I've packed in a lot of
rugged terrain in my time, but the Kayuga Pass matched
the toughest leather-skinned men I've ever encountered.
We had started out early that morning with over fifty
pounds on our backs, and by the time we broke camp, my
rifle felt like it weighed as much as an elephant's hide.
That's when it happened. Mac was the first to hear it, and
before long we all saw it.*

"Avalanche!" Mac called out.

*Rushing toward us was about twelve tons of hurtling
snow, and I knew Mac was a goner. I dropped my pack
and ran with my rifle to the side of the cliff. It was the last
thing I . . .*

Allegra threw the copy of *Trailblazer* down on her desk
that afternoon and smirked. "Oh, give me a break, will
you?" she said aloud. She looked at the cover, which
depicted a cartoon-style painting of a well-muscled man
hanging from a cable between two adjoining mountain
cliffs. "What trash."

She had bought the magazine on her way back from
lunch as a crazy lark. Now, after examining it, she was
more convinced than ever that Mark Trackman was stuck
permanently in a post-adolescent male hang-up. She
opened the magazine and peeked at the first page. There
was a letter from the editor, and next to it was a small
photo of Mark, staring into the camera with a fierce
expression. But it was the letter that caught her eye.

Dear Readers, [it said] *Our staff has journeyed all over
the world in order to bring you the most remarkable stories
of real men, stalwarts who have the courage and determination to go where most men would never dare trod.*

"Trod?" she said aloud. "There's no such word as

'trod'!" She flipped along further, noting page after page of true-life tales that vaguely resembled the exploits of a Paul Bunyan. In between the articles were ads for fishing gear, kayaks, various kinds of tents, and all manner of wilderness apparel.

Finally she threw the magazine down for good and glanced at the clock. The time had flown by while she had examined Mark Trackman's publication, and it was too late to make any calls. She stood up and stretched, looking around her office with a personal sense of satisfaction.

It consisted of two tiny rooms, and she made the maximum possible use of the space she had. The front room held two file cabinets, a desk, and a long table for assembling and stacking the issues of her newsletter. The back room, slightly larger, had been transformed into a kitchen and work area. A large gas stove, a freezer, a refrigerator, and a large central work table had been ingeniously arranged into the available space, giving her just enough room to move around. It was sometimes lonely because the small area did not allow enough room for more than one person to comfortably occupy the space at one time. Nevertheless, Allegra loved to cook, using it as a solace and an anchor when everything else seemed haywire. There was something basic and earthy about sinking her hands into fresh dough, or savoring the fragrance and clear colors of fresh vegetables. Today she had spent the better part of the afternoon putting the finishing touches to her contributions to Sabrina's party the following evening. With four dozen miniature quiches, a large container of marinated mushrooms, and a batch of large, luscious, old-fashioned oatmeal cookies studded with pecans and chocolate chips all packed and ready to go, she had plunked down at her desk as the sun was setting to take a look at the copy of *Trailblazer*. Now she was sorry she had spent so much time examining it. The sky outside was dark, and the building was quiet. She was probably the only one left. Lifting the magazine as if she were holding the tail of a dead mouse, she dropped it into the garbage, where it landed with a small thud.

"So long, Mac," she said aloud. "I hope you get off that mountain." Lugging the large canvas bag holding the food she had prepared, she turned out the lights and stepped into the hall. Locking the door behind her wasn't easy—it took several tries to get the bolt into place—but she was used to wrestling with it. So many things in the building needed fixing that she was accustomed to the inconveniences. Waiting for the elevator was another chore that required the patience of a saint.

As she pressed the button to go down, she noticed that the metal ashtray affixed to the wall was now hanging by one screw. She sighed, adjusted the canvas bag on her arm, and settled down for the long wait.

"Come on, come on," she muttered aloud as the ancient innards of the elevator clinked and rumbled into action. She had developed the odd habit of talking to the elevator to pass the time, and by now she had grown so used to her monologue that it seemed like a normal part of her daily routine. "You are a tortoise," she said. "Every day you get slower and slower." She punched the button again for good measure, even though she knew it would do no good. Finally, the elevator arrived, grinding to a lurching halt. "It's about time," she scolded. "I thought you'd never come."

The door opened with its usual creaks, revealing the figure of Mark Trackman, who was leaning casually against the wall of the car. "Really?" he said, grinning. "I had no idea I was expected."

"Mr. Trackman!" she exclaimed, fighting her embarrassment. "I didn't realize—I mean, I didn't think anyone was . . ." She trailed off and shrugged. "It doesn't matter what I mean." Deciding to ignore him, she walked into the elevator and pressed the button. Nothing happened.

"Now what's the matter?" she mumbled irritably.

"Are you addressing me or the elevator?" he asked. He strolled over to the buttons and pressed the one for the ground floor. Still nothing happened. "Looks like we might have to walk," he said.

Allegra's patience snapped. Before he could make a move, she punched the row of buttons with her fist. Mark flinched, eyeing her cautiously. "You have a mean right hook," he remarked, but his comment was cut short by the sudden jerking of the elevator into action. The doors closed, and the car began its descent.

Allegra smiled at him triumphantly, but her smile soured when the elevator suddenly jolted and stopped dead. She looked furiously at the panel of buttons and was about to strike them again, but an ominous puff of black smoke blew out from behind the board and she shrank back.

Mark fanned the smoke away and leaned forward to peer at the damage. "Looks like you've done it now," he said calmly. "I think it's shorted out."

"Oh, great. That's all I need." She watched as he tried the buttons one more time, but the elevator remained absolutely stuck. He tried the red emergency button next, but even that offered no help. The whole system appeared to have died.

"I'm afraid we've got something of a problem here," he said.

"I'll say," she retorted. "Doesn't anything in this place

work?" He had no answer and she sighed impatiently. "I guess we'll just have to wait for the janitor."

"There is no janitor," he said helpfully. "I had to let him go last month."

Allegra began to panic. She knew that they were the only people still in the building, and she was the only one who ever came in over the weekend. Today was Friday. Was she going to be stuck with him in an elevator all weekend? The thought was too grim to bear.

"Well, if we're going to be stuck here," he said, confirming her thought, "we might as well make the best of it." He slid down against the wall of the elevator and sat comfortably on the floor, crossing his long legs. Patting the floor with his hand, he offered her a seat next to him. "Come on," he said pleasantly. "I promise I won't bite."

Allegra sighed nervously. Being stuck in an elevator was no fun, but it was especially precarious to be stuck here with him. He was so completely masculine—and so very aware of it—that she wasn't sure she could handle being alone with him for too long. She staunchly disagreed with him on a major issue, but on the other hand, she found it hard to keep her eyes off him. It was a dangerous combination. He looked like a lion stretched out casually on the floor, a magnificent animal ready to protect or attack, whichever struck his fancy. But he was right about one thing. They should make the best of their situation. She put down the canvas bag with an air of resignation and plopped down next to him, pretending not to notice when their hands brushed. Several seconds passed before he spoke again.

"Mmmm," he said with interest. "Something smells good. Mind if I have a look?" Without waiting for an answer, he reached inside the bag and took out a round pan. Tearing off the silver foil, he held it up and looked at her for permission.

"Go ahead," she said dryly. "There's no reason to starve in here."

He took a bite and nodded appreciatively. "Not bad. What is this?"

"Something real men don't eat." She laughed. "Quiche."

"Well, this man thinks it's delicious." He shrugged, unfazed.

"Thank you," she answered, not knowing what else to say. She reached inside the bag and he watched delightedly as she took out the marinated mushrooms and the enormous, chewy cookies.

"Well, at least you came prepared," he said appreciatively.

"Isn't 'Be Prepared' the Boy Scout motto?" she asked slyly. She watched in awe as the mound of quiches rapidly diminished.

"I think so," he said between bites. "Are you implying that I'm an overgrown Boy Scout?"

"Listen, I'd really appreciate it if you wouldn't demolish all that food," she said nervously. "I'm supposed to bring it to a friend's party tomorrow night. Sabrina will understand if we eat some of it under the circumstances, but I'll never live it down if . . ."

His sharp eyes looked up. "Did you say Sabrina?" Allegra flushed. "Not Sabrina Melendey, the artist?" Allegra nodded dumbly. "Well, well," he said with a broad smile. "Isn't that a coincidence? I'm going to that very same party myself."

"Are you?" she said faintly. "I didn't know you were a friend of hers."

"Her husband once wrote a story for my magazine," he

explained briefly, but his eyes were twinkling. Did he think she had asked Sabrina to invite him? What a mortifying thought. He reached for the mushrooms. "Hey, these are great. What did you put on them, some kind of dressing?"

"They're marinated," she said, thinking that the major part of his diet probably consisted of hunks of meat and pizzas from the corner store. He gobbled several more mushrooms, and she shook her head. "Don't you ever eat?" she asked in protest. "You look as if you've been starving for days."

"Relax," he said. "I'm just packing it in so that I'll have a lot of energy later on. We may as well parcel out all of this stuff so that it will last all weekend, in case we need it."

"All weekend?" Allegra felt sick.

"Don't worry," he said heartily. "I know all about survival techniques."

"In an elevator?" she wailed. "Don't be ridiculous." She grabbed a cookie and bit into it, too distraught to care about depleting the supply. "This is all your fault, you know."

"*My* fault?"

"Of course. Nothing in this place works. I really shouldn't be surprised that we're trapped in here. I wouldn't be surprised if the whole building collapsed on our heads in another minute."

"Please, Ms. Russo. Or may I call you Allegra?"

"Why not?" she sighed. "I always insist on informality when I'm stuck in an elevator with someone."

"Good point. Please don't get hysterical, Allegra. It's highly inappropriate at the moment."

"Is that so?" She glared at him, munching furiously on the cookie. He was leaning casually against the wall, his long legs now stretched out in front of his lean, muscled body. His tawny head was cocked to one side, his clear golden eyes regarding her with unnerving confidence. He managed to be fully in control of the situation, despite the fact that he was seated on the floor of an elevator. Panic seemed a foreign emotion to him, and surely he would think of something. After all, he was a survival expert. If he could survive in a jungle, he could certainly connive a way to get out of an elevator.

"All right," she said at last, making her voice as level as possible. "I'm not hysterical."

He smiled briefly. "Good." He continued to munch, seemingly satisfied.

"Good? Is that all?" She turned to him in exasperation. "Aren't you going to get us out of here?"

"My dear Allegra," he said smoothly, "why be so dependent upon me? You spent the better part of yesterday afternoon convincing me that women are just as good as men. *You* get us out of here."

Allegra looked around at the four walls with utter desperation. She had absolutely no idea of how to proceed. But she knew that her helplessness was partly caused by the inner belief that he knew exactly what to do, and was merely baiting her. As soon as he was ready, he would stand up and magically get them out. She looked at Mark, who was biting into a cookie with obvious relish. He looked like a well-fed prep school boy without a care in the world. He also looked, more than ever, undeniably attractive. There was something about his careless attitude, his elegant posture, his aristocratic head, and the noble way he held it that gave him an aura of genuine presence. Mark was the kind of man who could turn heads without even trying. He could walk into a room without fanfare, but everyone would know he was there.

Stifling a sigh, Allegra stood up and walked to the doors. The building was utterly silent, but maybe someone downstairs would be able to hear if she yelled loud enough.

"Help!" she called at the top of her lungs. "Can anyone hear me?" Mark flinched and looked up sharply as she continued to holler into the silence. "Is anyone down there? We're stuck!" Her appeal was met by a weighty silence, during which Mark bit into another cookie and watched her with curious amusement.

"That's very ingenious of you," he offered affably. "I never would have thought of it."

"Why don't you make a suggestion, instead of sitting there and stuffing your face?" she demanded.

"Are you actually soliciting my opinion?" he asked.

"Yes! Would you please tell me how we're going to get out of here? I admit that I don't know how and that maybe you do. Please enlighten me. I know I'm only a feckless female, but with your unfathomable courage and my boundless admiration, surely we can find a way out of this mess."

He grinned and stood up lazily, wiping his fingers carelessly on his khaki trousers. "Now you're becoming irrational," he remarked with a sigh. "Oh, well. I guess I'll just have to confess. I really don't know any way out of here. Did you think I had access to some secret panel?" He shook his head. "I don't." Walking all around the perimeter of the small car, he examined the walls and then glanced up. "Unless we can find a way to climb up the shaft."

She followed his gaze and almost jumped in excitement. "Of course! You can climb up that cable to the next floor, pry the doors open, and walk out!"

"I can, can I?" he said, mocking her sudden confidence. "And just how am I going to get onto the roof of the car? Contrary to popular belief, I don't have the ability to leap tall buildings at a single bound." But the idea had intrigued him nonetheless. Allegra watched hopefully as he stared up at the ceiling, calculating silently. "No," he said after a moment, "I can't do it." He paused again. "But you can."

"Me!" she gasped.

"Of course you. I'll give you a lift and you can climb right up. The alternative is for you to give me a lift. Do you think you can handle that?"

Her expression changed as she considered his likely one hundred and seventy pounds. "Uh—no," she mumbled. "I guess not."

"Right. Then let's be logical. You now have the perfect opportunity to demonstrate your equality. Go on," he added in a friendly tone. "You can do it."

Encouraged, Allegra resolved to do as he suggested. After all, there was no other way to get out. She took a deep breath and faced him. "All right," she agreed. "Give me a boost."

His face changed quickly, so quickly that he was unable to hide the sudden admiration that was betrayed there. Allegra gave him a smile. "All set?" she asked.

He bent down and laced his hands together. Before she could give herself time to back down, she stepped onto the boost and pushed herself up. His hands immediately followed her, lifting her high into the air. She struggled to grab on to something and finally managed to grasp the metal bar that ran along the top of the car. Mark's strong arms held her easily, his hands anchored firmly and intimately around her hips. Allegra's thigh was lodged against him, the cotton folds of her dress bunched into the curve of his shoulder. Suddenly she was very grateful that she had worn stockings. Without their thin protection, her position would be more compromising than it already was.

His sensible voice interrupted her immodest thought. "Push the bar," he said helpfully.

She did, and found that it moved the panel that comprised the ceiling to one side. Staring upward, she saw the dark, dingy elevator shaft rising into the gloom. Mark lifted her further, his hands locked around her firm calves. She clasped the cable for support, holding it for dear life. With one more boost from below and a supreme effort on her part, she was out of the elevator car and in the dim regions of the shaft, peering down from her uneasy perch.

"Everything okay?" he asked cheerfully.

"Oh, fine. Just fine," she answered grimly. "God, it's filthy up here." Her knees, resting on top of the car, were immediately covered with an ugly layer of grime.

"This building is over a hundred years old," he called back. "What did you expect, new dirt?"

She glanced down at him and saw to her consternation that he was calmly biting into another cookie. Her dark eyes blazed, and as if in response, he looked up and waved. "Well?" he asked expectantly.

"Well, what?" she retorted.

"Aren't you going to start climbing?"

She squinted into the gloom, letting her eyes adjust. A ray of light showed from the upper floor, and Allegra calculated that it was only about seven feet away. Well, she thought, here goes nothing. She grabbed the cable as tightly as she could and found to her surprise that she was able to hoist herself up, inch by inch. The greasy cord left streaks between her legs, and her hands became raw and filthy, but she continued to pull herself up, using every ounce of energy she could summon. In no time at all she was out of breath and panting, but she wouldn't give up. After another inch and another pull she stopped to catch her breath and peek down into the car. Mark watched her slow climb with a look of encouragement on his face.

"Thata girl," he said, like a cheerleader at a game. "You're doing fine. Just catch the ledge there, and . . ."

She slipped suddenly and twisted out of control, her arms flailing into the air. Reaching out blindly, she grabbed the opposite cable and clung to it as her breath caught in her throat. Only then did she let out a sharp cry, partly from fear and partly from relief. She pressed her face against the greasy cord for a long moment, regained control, and then, in a final burst of energy, Allegra lunged toward the ledge marking the next floor.

"You made it!" he cried from below. "Can you open the doors?"

"I don't know," she gasped. "I'll try." She wedged her hand between the doors and realized she could pry them apart. The automatic device took over when the doors were opened a few inches, and then opened smoothly by themselves. In a moment she stood in the hall of the upper floor, safely out of danger.

"Whew!" she said, brushing herself off.

"What are you doing up there?" Mark called up, his voice echoing hollowly in the empty shaft.

"I'm just catching my breath," she called back. "That was quite a climb."

"Well, hurry up," he said impatiently. "I want to get out of here too."

She peered down to the elevator car and felt a stab of annoyance. Mark was sitting there calmly, munching a cookie and waiting leisurely to be rescued. "I hope you appreciate this," she couldn't resist calling down. "You didn't think I could do it, did you?"

He looked up, still chewing. "I thought you could. I just didn't think you would."

"And why not?"

"Because most people who complain a lot never do anything to help themselves."

"Complain!" she repeated, growing more aggravated. "And just what was I complaining about?"

"Look, Allegra," he said with infuriating nonchalance. "Let's not get into one of our famous discussions, all right? Just get me out of here. I have a lot to do tonight."

"You have a really rotten attitude, you know that?" she fumed. "I can't believe you. You purposely exude this macho man image, you pride yourself on survival techniques, and you depend on someone you won't even let into your precious club to get you out of an elevator!"

"My image, as you so kindly refer to it, seems to be mostly of your own making. I'm not really a 'macho man,' as you put it. I'm merely interested in adventure."

"Well, this is a great opportunity for you to have a wonderful adventure," she retorted, still smarting from his dismissal of her feat.

He looked up at her suspiciously. "What do you mean?"

"I mean, Mr. Adventure, that if I can do it, so can you." Allegra felt dangerously excited and daring, knowing that she was really about to do what she was thinking.

Mark knew it too. "Wait a minute," he protested, scrambling to his feet. "Don't—"

But Allegra didn't want to stay and listen. She knew that if she did, he would probably convince her to help him. Turning on her heel, she marched toward the stairwell and ran down the stairs and out of the building. She pictured Mark still trapped in the elevator, and as wicked as she knew it was, the thought amused her immensely. He would get out of there somehow, she was sure of it. After all, he was the survival expert.

Chapter Three

"And so I climbed out and left the building, leaving the self-sufficient Mr. Trackman to fend for himself," Allegra finished self-righteously. She helped herself to a bacon and spinach canape from a passing tray and popped it into her mouth with a smug expression as her two friends exchanged glances.

"I wonder if he got out," Veronica said, amazed.

"Well, you certainly left him with enough food," Sabrina added wryly. The three women stood in Sabrina's studio, an enormous but mostly empty SoHo loft, and the Mangia Society party was in full swing around them. The studio was often pressed into service for the Mangia Society because it was one of the few places large enough to hold the enthusiastic crowd. Allegra had started to feel guilty about asking her friend to accommodate the group so many times. It was one of the reasons the Mangia Society so desperately needed space of its own.

"Well, it looks like our little plan was foiled," Veronica said dryly, linking a conspiratorial arm around Sabrina.

Allegra's eyes narrowed suspiciously. She was beginning to feel perfectly justified in having left Mark Trackman in the elevator. Heaven only knew what would have happened if her two zany friends had had a chance to go to work on him.

"Colin will be so disappointed." Sabrina pouted.

"What will I be disappointed about?" Sabrina blinked guiltily as her husband strolled up next to her. He put an arm around her waist and nodded to Allegra and Veronica.

"Mr. Trackman can't make it tonight," Allegra explained, but Colin looked puzzled.

"Trackman?" he repeated, searching his memory. He looked at Sabrina for help. "I don't know about any Trackman coming."

"Oh, silly me," Sabrina said, trying to wangle out of it. "I forgot to tell you about him."

Allegra sighed emphatically. "Please," she pleaded with her friends. "Don't play Cupid for me, all right? I can't think of anyone less suited to me than Mark Trackman."

Colin lit up suddenly. "Mark Trackman! *Trailblazer* magazine? He's coming here?"

"Well, uh, no," Allegra broke in. She was hoping to get Colin off the subject, but Sabrina's husband was just warming up.

"I remember him," he continued brightly. "He's quite a nice guy. I wrote an article for him not too long ago. I'm thinking of doing another one as well."

Allegra blanched. "You are? You can't be serious. That magazine of his is a forum for macho men who like to show off." She giggled nastily. "And I bet the only people who read it are pale-faced weaklings hunched over their little desks in cramped little offices, dreaming of adventure."

"That's not true," Veronica spoke up. "My husband

reads the magazine sometimes." She grinned. "And he's no weakling."

"He certainly isn't," Colin agreed. "Men are faster and stronger. You can't deny that," he said.

"Women are just as capable," Veronica flared. "You're confusing sheer, brute force with the ability to accomplish something. Look at Dan," she continued, pouncing on the perfect example. "I'm proud to say that my husband just hired the first female firefighter on Point Lookout."

"That's right," said a voice behind her, "and she's the best cook we've ever had in the firehouse." They all turned to see Daniel Quincy standing and listening to their conversation, a glass of cold beer in one hand. His muscular frame sported a Point Lookout Volunteer Firemen T-shirt, and the amused grin on his darkly handsome face faded as he caught his wife's frown.

"That was a thoroughly tasteless remark," she said crushingly. "Why do you have to assume that cooking is a female domain? Some of the best chefs in the world are men."

"Score another point for the male side." Colin chuckled.

Veronica ignored him and pressed her point with Dan. "Just yesterday you told me she's the best firefighter you've seen in a long while."

Dan said nothing, wisely refraining from comment, but he and Colin exchanged glances of exaggerated patience that made their wives bristle.

"Now look what you've done," Allegra chided. "You're all going to go home and have arguments tonight, and all because of that stupid Mark Trackman."

"No one's going to argue," Sabrina said testily and in a voice that assured everyone that they all certainly would.

"It looks as if the Mangia Society is splitting into two warring factions," Allegra continued grimly. She turned accusingly to Dan and Colin. "And you two characters are the leading cause. You'd think this was Victorian England, the way you're carrying on."

"That's right," Sabrina said. "Women and men are equal under the law."

"Not according to the laws of nature," Colin said. "Men are physically stronger."

"What about endurance?" Veronica pressed. "It's a well-known fact that women excel at endurance."

Dan drained his beer glass and put it down with a decisive clink. "Okay," he said commandingly. "You want a contest? See if you can do this." Without warning, he wrapped a strong arm around Veronica and lifted her into the air. She squirmed helplessly, unable to wriggle out of his grasp, but Dan ignored her embarrassment. After a suitably dramatic pause, he strolled over to Sabrina and glanced at Colin. Colin nodded gleefully and they all watched as Dan wrapped his other arm around Sabrina.

"Oh, no, you don't," she warned, trying to twist away, but he was too fast for her. Everyone in the room laughed and applauded as the two women were both lifted up like trophies.

"Daniel Quincy," Veronica ordered. "You put me down this instant."

"I am warning you, Quincy," Sabrina fumed. "This is not the least bit amusing. Put me down!"

"I'll put you both down," he acquiesced, "when you admit I'm right."

Veronica reached down and picked up a half-filled glass of wine. Lifting it high over her husband's head, she said threateningly, "I'm warning you for the last time, chief." Very slowly she tilted the glass until the first few drops of wine spilled out and landed on top of Dan's head. By now everyone at the party had gathered to watch, and the women began to cheer Veronica on as the men laughed and hooted, clearly siding with Dan. Veronica turned the glass upside down, and wine splashed onto Dan's face, hair, and shirt. With a sharp cry of annoyance, he dropped the two women like hot potatoes and tried to brush the liquid from his face.

"Very funny," he huffed. "But you didn't prove a thing."

"Well, watch this." Allegra's tone was so adamant that everyone stared at her. Stalking over to Dan, she wrapped one determined arm around him and with great exertion managed to lift him a half an inch off the floor. Veronica was choking with laughter, and Sabrina was pointing merrily at Colin.

"Go for it, Allegra!" the hostess called out, and several female voices echoed her.

Allegra obligingly reached for Colin, who wore an expression of patronizing doubt. "You're going to hurt yourself," he began, but Allegra wasn't interested. By sheer dint of will, she lifted him as well and actually held him above the floor for one triumphant second before his left foot dragged on the ground.

The crowd watched this performance so intently that no one noticed the two newcomers enter the room. They all faced Allegra with their backs to the door, but Allegra looked up through her exertion, a man firmly locked under each arm, and in this decidedly undignified position she gazed into the unblinking eyes of Mark Trackman.

He stared back at her boldly, his eyes twinkling with sardonic amusement. "So, Ms. Russo," he said in a firm, clear voice that instantly dominated the room, "you're still trying to get yourself killed."

Heads swiveled as Dan and Colin were uncere-moniously dumped, and Mark strolled into the loft with a confident air. Wendell Croft, the elderly gentleman from the club, was with him, and he gave Allegra a courteous smile that managed to look elfin on his wizened features. She looked back and forth between the two of them with a wild, dazed expression on her face.

"How—how did you ever get out?" she stammered.

Mark sauntered over and stood next to her, looking down at her flushed face with lordly good humor. "Elementary, my dear Allegra. That elevator has its quirks, but it always starts again after a while. You were in such a hurry to leave that I didn't have a chance to stop you."

Her mouth fell open. "But why didn't you tell me that?"

"And spoil your heroic efforts?" He shook his head. "Oh, no. You were so busy proving yourself that I didn't have the heart to put a damper on your spirit. Besides, you left me with such a tasty repast that I really was in no hurry to leave." He brushed a tiny speck of lint from his sleeve and she stared at him speechlessly. Mark was dazzling in a beautifully tailored tuxedo, complete with studs and a starched black bow tie. He and Wendell were the only men at the party dressed so formally, but they didn't look at all out of place. They looked stunning.

As Allegra gasped and caught her breath, Colin regained his composure and stepped forward to greet his new guests. "Mr. Trackman, I presume?"

Mark nodded, coolly ignoring Allegra, and shook Colin's hand. "May I present my friend, Mr. Wendell Croft? I hope you don't mind my bringing him."

"Not at all." Colin beamed. "The more the merrier."

Sabrina wound an arm through her husband's and gave Mark a charming smile. "So you're Mark Trackman. Very nice." The last words were spoken with deliberate emphasis, making Allegra want to sink through the floor.

"Let's have a look," Veronica chimed in, giving Mark a not-to-subtle once-over. "Oh, yes, we were right. Very nice indeed."

Mark bore the feminine scrutiny without flinching. "I must say, Allegra, your friends certainly know how to make a man feel welcome." Allegra thought she saw the beginning of a smile teasing the corners of his mouth, but she wasn't sure.

"Thank you," Sabrina said graciously. "Colin, why don't you introduce Mr. Trackman to everyone?" She turned back to Mark. "We're so glad you could make it."

"I almost didn't," he answered, staring jovially at Allegra.

Sabrina pretended to ignore the electricity and touched her husband's elbow, prodding him forward. "Go ahead, dear," she said, her gentle voice underlined with a command. "There are a number of people here who would like to meet him. Of course," she added with a little flutter of laughter, "he's already met Allegra."

Colin stepped forward obligingly and led Mark away. "Indeed I have met Allegra," Mark said as he moved away. "She's . . ." The remainder of his sentence was lost in the crowd, and Allegra frowned. She had to admit she would have liked to have heard what he was going to say about her. The impact of his entrance lingered, and a small but weighted silence settled between her and her friends.

"Well," Sabrina said at last with a sly grin, "we were right on the nose. What a hunk!"

"Sabrina!" Veronica laughed. "You have a very limited vocabulary when it comes to men."

"Well, how would you describe him?" Sabrina turned her large green eyes on her friend with mock innocence.

Veronica thought for a few seconds, and then a smile lit up her face and she nodded emphatically. Sabrina laughed, and they said in unison, "A hunk!"

Allegra sighed in a futile effort to hide her reactions.

"You two are insufferable," she said. "You have to admit, the man is exactly as I described him."

"Oh, sure," Veronica said with broad sarcasm. "A grizzly bear with two teeth missing, carrying a club." She stole a glance at Mark, whose strikingly handsome golden-brown head was visible across the room. "Fat chance," she concluded dryly.

Sabrina dropped her teasing facade. "When are you going to cut this out, Allegra?" she demanded. "That man is absolutely gorgeous, and you know it. If his attitude is a little superior, well, it's your job to change it. Men are never perfect, you know. They all need a little training."

Veronica smirked, but Allegra was looking at the floor. "Okay," she said quietly. "I admit he's attractive." She looked up. "But he really is impossible. You should have heard the way he talked to me yesterday. It was really unbelievable. He's . . ."

"Oh, boy." Sabrina shook her head. "This girl's got it bad. That man really intrigues you, doesn't he?" She looked at Veronica. "This is more serious than we thought."

Veronica nodded thoughtfully. "Apparently so."

Allegra was beginning to feel like a bird trapped in a cage. She followed Mark's progress across the room, watching him charm one person after another. He was absolutely magnetic, and there was something about him that made her tingle with anticipation. In anticipation of what, she didn't know. She knew only that something about him made her blood jump.

A slight frown creased her forehead as she excused herself and drifted away from her friends. Maybe they were right, despite all their teasing. Maybe she was running away from an attraction that threatened to overpower her if she let it. She maneuvered toward the kitchen, the one place where she could be sure of sorting out her thoughts. The new batch of miniature quiches she had prepared at home for the party were ready to come out of Sabrina's oven. Allegra always found solace in the simple, methodical details of cooking which calmed and enabled her to think logically.

Sure enough, a peep inside the oven assured her that the quiches were done. She expertly slid the tray out and turned around to head for the opposite counter just as someone came through the swinging doors.

"Hi, Zeebo," she said, looking him up and down. He was dressed in a black-and-red-plaid shirt with black trousers and wide black suspenders. An independently wealthy young man, Zeebo had recently gone into business as an art agent, with Sabrina as his first client. "You're looking dapper, as always."

Zeebo made a beeline for the quiches and popped one into his mouth. "I knew you'd come in here." She grinned. "You're never far behind the food."

He munched happily and nodded. "You do have good taste, Allegra," he said in his nasal, collegiate voice. "And I'm not just talking about the quiche." He gestured with his curly head toward the door. "That Trackman fellow is quite a guy." He smiled knowingly. "Then again, I hear you're pretty tough yourself. Trackman was just telling me about that feat you pulled off in the elevator."

"Is that so?" she hedged, busying herself with the food.

"I must admit, it didn't surprise me," he continued. "You've always been quite enterprising, you know. Who else could have gotten the Mangia Society off the ground? Yes," he concluded, nodding sagely, "you two are a very good match indeed."

Allegra almost choked. "Did Sabrina put you up to this?" she demanded, turning to face him.

Zeebo didn't flinch. "Up to what?"

Before she could answer, a small, intense Japanese man popped into the kitchen. "Oh, sorry," he said immediately. "I was looking for Sabrina."

"Hello, Mishi," Allegra greeted him. "Wait a minute, don't go away empty-handed." She handed him the tray of quiches.

He took it and started to leave but turned back to add, "Say, that Trackman fellow—he's a boyfriend of yours?"

Allegra threw up her arms. "What is this, a conspiracy?"

Mishi grinned and backed through the swinging doors just as a ruddy-faced man in a postman's uniform came through. The newcomer waved casually to Zeebo and headed for the refrigerator.

"What are you looking for, Sal?" Allegra asked.

"I just want to get a beer," he answered briefly, rummaging through the crowded refrigerator. "Some guy out there is telling this terrific story about camping out in a South American rain forest surrounded by headhunters, and I don't want to miss it." He found a can of beer, popped it open, and took a long swallow before going back to the party.

"It's Grand Central Station in here," Allegra remarked to Zeebo, who was still lounging against the wall.

"You'll have to excuse me," he said with a smile. "I don't want to miss that story myself." The smile lingered for a second longer than was necessary, and she pointed toward the doors.

"Out!" she commanded. "If I hear one more insinuation about Mark Trackman, I'm going to scream."

He held up a hand in defense. "Okay, okay," he said. "Don't bother showing me out, I know the way." He vanished quickly, but not before flashing her another one of his teasing grins.

Alone in the tiny kitchen, Allegra busied herself with various small tasks, but she couldn't escape the merry laughter from the party. She wondered just what Mark was doing now, who he was talking to and how he was responding. She couldn't help but remember the feminine signs of approval that had been evident from the moment he had made his entrance. All her friends seemed to know something she didn't. As she poured herself a glass of wine, she admitted to herself that Mark Trackman was indeed quite a catch. He only had to be tamed.

Several moments of relative quiet emanated from the party, and Allegra grew curious. After a few more minutes she decided to investigate the situation when a sudden burst of laughter and a round of applause interrupted her thoughts. After another sprinkling of laughter she opened the swinging door a crack to look through. Everyone at the party was gathered around Mark, who was telling some kind of story.

"And that's how it ended," he was saying with the polished relish of a born storyteller. "My men and I trudged out of the Amazon forest and back to civilization with our heads intact. Or, as one of my colleagues put it, my hat size remained the same."

Everyone laughed again, enjoying the impromptu entertainment. Two women clad in sophisticated cocktail dresses saw Allegra peeking through the doors, and they rushed toward her. Not wanting to be caught like a child who has snuck out of bed to watch her parents' party, Allegra stepped out and greeted the two Mangia Society members.

"Hello, Mitzi, hello, Carla. How are you?"

Mitzi had only one thing on her mind, and she wasted no time at all. "I hear you know that Trackman fellow," she said, pinning Allegra with an intent gaze.

"Well, yes . . ."

"I want him, Allegra."

Allegra blinked. "What?"

"You heard me. That is the most gorgeous specimen of male I have ever laid eyes on. I want you to introduce me. What a hunk!"

"The female members of this club have a very limited vocabulary when it comes to men." Allegra sighed.

"That man is probably the best catch in the whole room, do you know that?" Carla remarked with interest. They all turned to look at Mark, who was now engaged in conversation with Dan and Colin across the room. As if on cue, he looked up and saw them, nodding briefly in greeting. His eyes sparkled with an inner enjoyment that did not escape any of the three women watching.

"He's looking right at me." Mitzi tittered.

"Well, why don't you pursue him?" Allegra suggested finally. "He seems to like the subject of hunting."

Mitzi considered this comment for a moment before making up her mind. "You're right," she said, and started toward the opposite side of the room.

"Way to go, Mitzi," Carla murmured as they watched her take his arm and corral him into a corner.

Allegra stood rooted to the spot as Mitzi smiled up at Mark, clinging to his arm. She couldn't tell what Mark's reaction to her friend was. He merely nodded and offered an occasional reply, but the expression on his face was decidedly neutral. Allegra decided not to stand around gawking. She tore herself away from the scene and went back into the kitchen, where, to her chagrin, black smoke seeped out of the oven.

She quickly opened the oven door and turned off the heat, groaning as she surveyed the last batch of quiches. They were burnt to a crisp.

"It smells like a forest fire in here," said a sardonic and familiar voice behind her. She wheeled around, completely flustered, and encountered the bemused and rather world-weary face of Mark Trackman. The door behind him was still swinging forcefully, as if to help air out the smoke, and he peered down at the smoldering quiches curiously. "Burnt offerings," he commented.

"They look like shrunken heads," she agreed with a nervous laugh. To hide her profound embarrassment, she whisked the pan over to the garbage and unceremoniously dumped the blackened quiches. What on earth must he think of her? She was supposed to be a food expert and a great cook, and here she was scraping a culinary disaster into the garbage.

Mark watched her avidly, as if he were about to make some smart remark, but he kept silent and waited as she composed herself.

"Well," she said after a long moment, picking up the glass of wine she had left on the counter, "that wasn't so bad after all."

"It wasn't?"

"Of course not," she said evenly. "The secret of a great cook is knowing how to handle all situations, including emergencies. Anyone can handle a triumph, isn't that true?"

He laughed appreciatively. "I suppose so. I never thought of it that way."

Allegra relaxed a little. Apparently he wasn't planning to bait her. "Having a good time?" she asked conversationally.

"It's a jungle out there," he answered. "I was cornered by a maniacal woman who didn't want to let me go."

Allegra smiled. "How did you ever escape?"

"I'm an escape artist, remember?"

"Yes," she laughed, "and elevators are your specialty."

"This is the craziest party I've ever been to," he added in a confiding tone. "I've never seen such an eclectic blend of people. I met a fireman, a Japanese filmmaker, a cabdriver, a mailman, the vice-president of a bank, and a famous artist, all in the last thirty minutes."

Allegra nodded cheerfully. "That's the Mangia Society," she said proudly. "We don't have any restrictions. That's one of the reasons why our club has been such a success."

Mark lifted an eyebrow. "Was that a small dig?" he asked, a trace of his former haughtiness returning.

She smiled impishly and nodded. "I couldn't help it," she said.

"Well, it so happens that the Gotham Men's Club is also very liberal, in its own way," he went on. "In its heyday, anyone with a taste for adventure was welcome. I know it sounds less than meaningful today, but back then most gentlemen's clubs had very strict social rules. Being allowed to join was considered an honor and a privilege."

"Well, obviously, your philosophy hasn't been working lately," she said seriously. "You're about to go broke."

"I know," he said. "But there's not much we can do."

"You can rent me the space I need. That would help."

He looked down at her, his tawny eyes capturing hers and holding them. "Not really, Allegra. It would only be a drop in the bucket, I'm afraid." He spoke quietly, but she felt a sudden, invisible cord between them, as if an intangible force was now drawing them together. She knew it would last for as long as he continued to look at her like that, and at that moment, she felt perfectly content to stand there forever, gazing into his eyes. But the spell was broken as Sabrina popped into the kitchen.

"Oops!" she said at once, her hand covering her mouth. She disappeared as quickly as she had come, and Mark laughed.

"Do you get the feeling there's some kind of conspiracy going on here?" Mark asked.

Allegra looked down at the floor, not yet ready to admit what everyone else already seemed to know. She started suddenly as she felt his hands on her arms. He held her gently but firmly, compelling her to look up. She did, her face brimming with a crazy tumble of emotions. Their eyes met again, and this time the look that passed between them was charged with an intensity that seemed to have a physical effect on her. She trembled, mesmerized by the linear beauty of his face, knowing that any second she would embark on an adventure that even Mark Trackman would find tantalizing.

"Everyone here seems to think there's something going on between us," he continued in a husky voice.

"Do they?" She was stalling, wanting to prolong this

moment and yet afraid to surrender to the torrent she knew lay in waiting.

He responded with a question of his own, one far more provocative. "Is there, Allegra? Is there something between us, or do you really hate the ground I walk on?"

"I don't hate you," she breathed. "You know that."

"If there is something between us, then I think it's high time we found out about it." His arms went around her, drawing her close, and a bolt of lightning went through her. His body was lean and hard and muscular, and she was aware of every deliciously masculine inch of it. His head, sporting the golden-brown mane she had secretly admired, bent in a delicate gesture, and she lifted her face to his. In another moment they were kissing, and Allegra could hardly bear the excitement of it. For so long, for so very long, this man had been haunting the secret places of her mind, and actually being in his arms was like finally tasting a wildly desirable forbidden fruit that had been denied her.

But the intoxicating newness of emotion was only the beginning. She had feared that his kiss might be arrogant, or brutal, or simply unappetizing—the kiss of a caveman bearing down on a hapless woman with elemental force. Instead, he took her mouth with exquisite gentleness, letting the sensation linger and envelop them both. Instinctively she knew that any man who could kiss her like this would be a tremendous lover, and the thought somehow drew her arms up and around his neck. He responded at once, covering her face with countless smaller kisses that sent little tremors all through her body. Allegra felt her heartbeat quicken and she was aware of the enticingly masculine scent of him. Her eyes closed and her head thrown back, Allegra seemed to see and hear and feel everything at that moment. She was lost in a private world that consisted only of the two of them.

He found her mouth again, this time parting her lips with his tongue and finding his way inside. The room began to swirl around them, and they clung to each other, dizzy with the newfound awareness of what they had discovered. If she had ever entertained any doubts about Mark's attitude toward women, they were now being banished and swept away under the tide of sensation that traveled between them. There was absolutely no way Mark could not respond to what was touching and softening his heart. The physical sensation was tinged with so much sweetness and such a painfully gentle swell of longing that Allegra knew she would never forget this moment. No matter what happened between them, she would cling to the memory of this first kiss for a long time to come.

A sudden knock on the door interrupted them, and Allegra opened her eyes with reluctance. The kitchen was there around her even though she didn't want to acknowledge it. Mark had the same dreamy look on his face, and their foreheads touched briefly as they each caught their breath.

"Who is it?" Mark asked.

"It's me," Zeebo answered on the other side. "I think the two of you should join the conversation out here. It's getting extremely interesting, and it concerns you."

Mark and Allegra exchanged looks of curiosity but they were slow to react. Allegra didn't want to float back down to earth yet because she knew she would be very confused when she did. Just what was she starting here with Mark Trackman? A few minutes ago she had sworn that they were worlds apart.

The sound of loud voices reached their ears, and they

realized that some sort of argument was erupting at the party. Zeebo had said it concerned them.

"I guess we'd better see what's going on," Allegra whispered, looking up at Mark. She wanted to look at him forever, even though she was afraid of what it might do to her. He nodded, still holding her, obviously as hypnotized as she was.

They emerged through the swinging doors into a heated forum that had erased the previously relaxed mood of the Mangia Society gathering.

"Women are known for their superior endurance," Veronica was saying disparagingly. "It's a proven fact."

"What, back to this again?" Allegra asked, startled. "What's going on here?"

"Your little stunt has captured the fancy of the group," Colin answered dryly. "Everyone is talking about it."

"*My* little stunt?" she repeated, dumbfounded. "Dan was the one who started it."

"Me?" Dan looked amazed. "You kept insisting that women are equal, and you were hell-bent on proving it. You should have been here, Mark," he added, turning instinctively to face his most assured ally. "That magazine of yours really had her riled."

Allegra blanched, and Mark's face lit up with an amused grin. "Really?" he asked congenially. "I had no idea I was so influential. I must say, I'm flattered." He took Allegra by the arms and turned her around to face him. Taking her face in his hands, he looked down at her flushed countenance. "Do I really have that much of an effect on you?" he asked with interest.

Allegra squirmed out of his grasp. How could he joke after what had just happened between them? The few moments in the kitchen had been so private and lovely, but they were now rudely interrupted by a ludicrous argument. She needed time to sort out her thoughts.

The entire group watched her. Facing them with dignity, Allegra announced, "This whole discussion is getting out of hand. If all of you want a challenge, then I suggest you invent a sensible one, instead of standing here and arguing about it. The Mangia Society has been through a lot, but I've never seen it divided into two warring factions—male versus female. It's so primitive."

"I love primitive," Colin interjected with relish. "It's right up my alley."

"Don't be such a pill, Allegra," Sabrina added. "It's still a friendly argument." She turned to her husband for confirmation, and he nodded.

"Well . . ." Allegra was at a loss for words, but Mark was not.

"I think a little competition is a good idea," he said unexpectedly. "It separates the men from the boys, and," he did not hesitate to add pointedly, "the women from the girls, so to speak."

"But it seems so antagonistic!" Allegra protested.

"Nonsense," Zeebo said briskly. "That's just the trouble with women. They don't like to face confrontation. They're always wriggling out of things."

"We are not!" Allegra cried, seized by a sudden flash of anger. What was going on here? "And we don't have to prove it to you!"

Mark's hand touched her arm, sending an unwelcome surge of heat through her body. She shut her eyes for an instant, willing the reaction to go away, but it didn't. She had never been so confused in her life.

Suddenly, a dry and pleasant voice was heard above all others. "May I offer a suggestion?"

Allegra opened her eyes and saw Wendell standing in

the center of the room, addressing everyone with stately confidence.

"Please do," Sabrina urged.

Wendell's small but elegant frame commanded attention as he held up a hand. The mumbling in the room died down and finally ended in an expectant hush. "Ahem," he began, confirming his authority. No one intervened. "Now then." He clasped his hands behind his back and faced them squarely. "This has been a remarkable evening," he said. His voice was pitched low, but it dominated every corner of the loft. "It offers a unique opportunity to engage in the sort of adventure that is all too often lacking in the hustle and bustle of modern life." He paused, surveying the group of much younger people, and saw that they were interested, curious, and waiting respectfully for him to continue. "Many years ago, when I was in training with the group that came to be known as Teddy's Raiders, we had an ingenious method of testing our mettle and having fun at the same time." Again he paused, this time with a sense of drama, as the group waited to hear what he had to say. "I propose a contest," he announced. "One that will include everyone who wishes to participate. One, I hasten to add, that is fair and equitable to both sexes."

They all looked at each other in anticipation as excitement passed through the crowd. Wendell's face became enlivened with the certainty that what he was about to propose would be truly inspiring. Allegra glanced at Mark out of the corner of her eye and noted with a flutter of emotion that his face held unmistakable affection. Wendell drew himself up with impeccable dignity, and Mark seemed to unconsciously follow the example. He stood erect and proud, waiting to hear what Wendell was going to offer.

"A scavenger hunt!" Wendell said with a flourish.

A crescendo built immediately throughout the room as this information was absorbed and evaluated. Eyes were sparkling and heads were nodding, but Wendell held up his hand once again to gain their attention. The buzz died at once as the group turned eagerly to hear the rest of his scheme.

"It will be divided between brain and brawn," he stated with a wry smile. "An even match of will, wit, and endurance."

"It's very intriguing," Allegra admitted slowly.

Sabrina giggled suddenly. "Sounds like fun." She peeked at Colin, who was standing behind her.

"Okay by me." He nodded thoughtfully. "Count me in."

"And me," Dan added immediately.

"Me too!" Veronica chimed.

The others in the room added their assent to the plan, and slowly, as the excitement grew, the crowd divided up like groups at a junior high school dance. All the men congregated on one side, and the women gathered opposite them. Two teams were born as they faced each other, prepared to compete. Wendell remained stationary during this transition, watching with knowing amusement as the eager chatter continued.

"Ahem!" he said after a few minutes, commanding their attention once again. Wendell obviously had more to say, and the crowd listened with new interest. "If there are no objections, I will compose the list of required items." He waited politely to see if anyone would object, but no one did. Allegra instinctively trusted him even though she barely knew him because Wendell was clearly an honorable man who, she felt, knew more than he was revealing about this contest. Something told her that if she went along with him, she would be pleasantly surprised by the contest's outcome.

"Good," Wendell said, satisfied that they all agreed. "Now, the list will consist of a variety of items, ranging from the simple to the more intricate. Finding everything on the list will constitute the 'brain' part of the hunt."

Allegra smiled, already caught up in the spirit of the hunt. She whispered with Sabrina, Veronica and several other women, and then they quickly divided themselves into subteams. Across the room, the men planned similar strategies, though Allegra didn't concern herself with them. A fierce desire to win this contest had swiftly overtaken her, and she concentrated on the procedure as Wendell outlined the next part of the hunt.

"Boys and girls," he said dryly, holding up a hand to silence them. "Allow me to proceed to the 'brawn' part of the contest. The endurance race."

"Race?" she echoed.

Wendell looked directly at her. "Yes, a race," he repeated, "with just one catch." He smiled before continuing. "Yes," he murmured to himself, "this is perfect." He spoke clearly, making sure both teams understood. "The race will be point to point. That means it will start here in New York, but it will continue into the Catskill Mountains, reversing itself at Bear Mountain and returning back to the city. The finish line will be the entrance to the Gotham Men's Club."

"Where the winners will parade inside!" Allegra couldn't resist saying.

He smiled calmly. "If you like. But let me explain the purpose of the trek to Bear Mountain."

"I know!" Mark said suddenly. "We have to get the things on the list along the way, right?"

Wendell smiled at him fondly. "That's correct. I

myself will plant some of the items on the trail so that I know you have followed it properly. The final item will be at the very top of the mountain, and it will be the only item of which there is only one. Only one of the teams will be able to get it."

A low murmur spread as this piece of information was absorbed. Allegra's eyes were shining when she looked across the room at Mark. He was watching her and she couldn't determine if the bemused look on his face was one of levity or affection.

"The final night," Wendell continued in his dry but authoritative voice, "will be a sleep-over."

"Sleep-over?" Sabrina gulped. "You mean in sleeping bags? On the ground?"

"Camping out," Wendell confirmed, "on Bear Mountain."

Sabrina gulped, but Allegra felt exhilarated. A competitive spirit she never knew she possessed rapidly surfaced, and she relished the powerful energy it gave her. Veronica looked as excited as she felt, and the two of them exchanged an enthusiastic glance.

"Uh—I've got a confession to make," Sabrina whispered suddenly. "I'm not a woods person. Central Park, maybe, but not camping out. I think I'm allergic to trees, and grass makes me itch." She shot a baleful look at Colin, who had been on countless expeditions in search of fossils.

He caught the look and smiled wickedly. "My wife jumps at the sound of crickets," he announced to her chagrin.

"I do not," she protested. "I just don't like the idea of stepping on something in the night that either squeaks or squishes. Especially if I'm barefoot, which I usually am."

Colin laughed behind his hands, and Mark chuckled

out loud. "Once when we were in a cabin in the country," Colin recounted, "Sabrina stepped on a slug. You could have heard her scream all the way back in New York."

"So I hate slugs!" she exclaimed, flaring. "So what?"

"Oh, I hate them too," he mimicked. "Yechy, slimy creatures. Ugh!" Mark and Dan and the other men roared with laughter, but Allegra stepped forward with a look on her face that silenced their mirth at once.

"You can laugh all you want," she said sternly. "But I assure you, you're in for some big surprises."

Mark eyed her admiringly. "I don't doubt it," he said. "You've surprised me a great deal already."

Allegra wasn't quite sure how to interpret his comment, so she chose the most graceful way that came to mind. "Thank you," she said with cool poise. "I'm glad you noticed."

"Now, now," Wendell interrupted smoothly, "let's not get testy over this. Just hope that everyone who starts the course finishes it. I'll be at the top of the mountain to be sure of that." He stopped and thought for a moment, and then a big smile lit up his face. "Yes, yes." He chuckled to himself, laughing at some private joke. He looked around the room decisively. "That's it for the rules. I'll go into the next room and make up the list." He strode through the assembled group without further comment, purposefully heading around the corner of the L-shaped loft.

Mark took the opportunity to catch Allegra's attention. "Oh, Ms. Russo," he called. "Care for a side bet?"

She glared at him. "Name it!"

"If the men win, you have to cook a Saturday night meal for the Gotham Men's Club every week for a year."

Her eyebrows went up. "Oh, I couldn't do that, Mr. Trackman."

"Why not?"

"Because women aren't allowed inside," she answered airily.

"So we'll make an exception." His tone was loaded with challenge, and she couldn't back down.

"Fair enough," she agreed. "But if you lose—"

"We won't."

"If you lose," she repeated, ignoring the interruption, "you have to rent me the third floor of the club."

"Agreed," he said at once, adding under his breath, "and may the best man win."

Chapter Four

"Quiet, everyone! Quiet!" Sabrina clapped her hands for attention in the middle of the loft. "We're ready to begin!" she called as the group assembled once again.

The room slowly quieted down as Wendell joined Sabrina in the center of the room. He held a sheaf of papers and looked over one copy of his list as he waited for the group to settle down.

"There are a few items you may have difficulty with," he began when he had their attention. "Then again," he added thoughtfully, looking up at Allegra, "you may not."

Allegra looked quizzically at Sabrina, who merely shrugged. She stole a glance at Colin and Mark, noting that they looked just as eager as she felt. Over fifty people waited in hushed anticipation, but before Wendell could continue, there was a subtle migration among the sexes. As before, the two teams faced each other with determination.

"Round one!" Allegra announced merrily as she joined the other women. Wendell, the ringleader of the spirited crowd, looked up patiently and waited for the last few stragglers to take sides.

"Are we all settled, boys and girls?" he asked pleasantly. After a few titters everyone listened excitedly.

"Good, then let's begin." He leaned on his cane for support as he perused the list. "A two-day scavenger hunt," he announced.

"Three days?" Carla moaned. "I have to be at work on Monday morning."

"Call in sick!" Sal called back from across the room.

"No way." Mitzi pouted. "Count me out."

"Me too."

"And me."

People began to break ranks, straying to the back of the room to listen, no longer participating.

Wendell was quick to counter. "Everyone may contribute as much time as he or she wishes," he explained. "Be so good as to let me outline the entire procedure. The whole nature of the game is based on compromise."

Everyone looked up, ready to hear him out. He beamed, pleased with the attentive attitude of his audience. "There are a number of items to be gathered, and there are tasks to complete. It doesn't matter who or how many accomplish the gathering, what matters is which team ultimately wins. After all," he added with a benevolent smile, "isn't the object of the game to determine which is the stronger sex?"

A low hum of agreement spread across the room. Allegra felt charged by the excitement around her, and her eyes sparkled with the competitive spirit that was building. She found herself stealing another glance at Mark, who looked more contemplative than challenged. His aristocratic face was lost in thought, as if he were mapping out the race bit by bit, calculating each team's strengths and weaknesses. Allegra stared at him in awe. He was electric in his concentration.

Suddenly Mark broke from his trance and looked up, gazing directly at her. She was so startled that she almost gasped. His golden-brown eyes bored into her, as if he easily read and dissected every one of her thoughts. Allegra's lively face was a contrast in moods: her olive complexion was flushed with high color, and her dark eyes were punctuated with bright sparkles. The man across the room was absolutely magnetic, but Allegra was determined to accomplish her goal. Mark stared back at her coolly, his sharp eyes watching her every move and though he seemed like a lion ready to pounce, she was as fearless and proud in her iron stubbornness. If only the memory of the way he had held her during those precious, timeless seconds that had seemed like a drop of eternity would not intrude on her single-mindedness she could be assured of her superiority. Her molten attraction to Mark lingered just beneath her smooth surface, and her eyes blazed as she fought to keep it under control.

Wendell's dry voice broke her reverie. "The items on the list can be found between here and the summit of Bear Mountain," he said. "In order to find the last item at the top of the mountain, it will be necessary to hike the Adirondack Trail, starting at the parking lot at the Bear Mountain Inn. I will have planted clues along the trail that will lead you to the exact spot. Of course, it will also be necessary to camp out overnight. Not only is this contest partly a test of endurance, but some of the items can be found *only* at night, in that particular locale."

"Count me in on that," Veronica said eagerly.

"Me too," Sabrina added, throwing caution to the winds. Her friends looked at her in surprise, and her husband smirked. "Well, I don't care," she insisted. "It sounds like fun."

"What if there are slugs?" Colin teased mercilessly.

"Slugs or no slugs," Allegra broke in firmly, "we are going to win!"

"That's the spirit!" Veronica said. She stepped forward to get her copy of the list, and the others followed suit, pressing toward Wendell with alacrity. Suddenly no one wanted to waste a single moment of time, and the room was overtaken with a sense of madcap adventure.

Wendell distributed copies of the list as fast as he was able to, and the pieces of paper practically flew out of his hands. "It is now ten o'clock!" he called out over the din. "You have forty-eight hours in which to gather the items on the list, If you're late, you'll be automatically disqualified. Happy hunting, and tally ho!"

Allegra stood to one side, examining her copy of the list with avid interest. The very first item took her by surprise. It was the recipe for the trout mousse at *La Grande Mer*, the restaurant where she and her friends had lunched the day before. She looked at Wendell in surprise, and he smiled knowingly.

"How did you know?" she asked in awe.

"Oh, someone mentioned something about it," he answered with a grin that told her just how sharp he really was. "I tried to include a little bit of everything to suit everyone's strengths."

She nodded, impressed. But she still didn't know how she was going to get that recipe. Wendell was even more clever than she had thought.

"Say, look at this!" Mark exclaimed, looking delightedly at Wendell. "Why, you crafty devil. No wonder we have to camp out at night."

Colin ran up next to him and examined the item that Mark was pointing to. "Fireflies!" He laughed. "Of course. You can only see them when they light up at night."

"And you can only find them in the Catskills this early in the season," Wendell added, pleased at his choice.

" 'A metal entrance button to the Museum of Natural History,' " Mitzi read aloud from the list. She frowned, not understanding. But Colin smiled in triumph and removed a small tin button sporting a picture of a dinosaur from his pocket. He held it up with a grin and announced, "I work there. Item one—check!"

But his smugness was short-lived as Sabrina dug in her handbag and removed an identical button. "Not so fast, Colin," she said gleefully. "Don't forget, I married my way in."

Allegra's excitement mounted as she glanced at all of the items. Some were relatively easy to get, but some were true rarities. The contest would take skill as well as persistence. Where were they going to find an old Jax beer bottle? Or a two-dollar bill?

Veronica was less interested in the list and more interested in winning. "Come on, you two slowpokes," she cajoled. "Let's get cracking."

Allegra and Sabrina shot into action, sprinting behind Veronica toward the door. They clattered down the stairs and huddled together on the sidewalk, dividing up the list among the entire women's team. The rest of the group broke up and frantically hailed cabs or ran for cars. Husbands and wives fought for control of vehicles, and in no time at all a traffic jam had materialized in front of the building.

"This is a madhouse," Allegra said, looking around at the confusion. Horns honked rudely and arguments erupted as everyone tried to push through. "Let's get going," she said firmly. "Where's Veronica? Veronica!"

"Over here!" Veronica called from across the street. She dangled her car keys from one finger as Sabrina climbed into Dan and Veronica's station wagon. "Hurry up!"

"In a minute!" Allegra called back as her eye spotted a car that she had often seen parked near the club. The license plate read EXPLORE. "I just found one of the items on the list!"

Three men overheard her, but it was too late. She wrested the hood ornament from the parked Alfa Romeo and slipped it into her purse as Veronica lurched out of the parking space and pulled over to pick her up. "Come on, Allegra," she said urgently. "They're coming."

Allegra jumped into the backseat of the station wagon like a bank robber escaping from a holdup just as Dan Quincy appeared, followed by Mark and Colin. He lunged directly in front of the car, daring Veronica to stop him, and she had no choice but to hit the breaks. The car screeched to a halt, and she threw her head out of the window.

"Out of my way!" she yelled.

"This is my car too," he protested, refusing to back down.

"Hey, Dan!" It was Mark's voice. "Let them have it. We'll go in style," he added, pointing to his car.

"Nice wheels, Trackman," Dan said admiringly. He smiled at his wife, who was still behind the wheel of their station wagon. "Okay, Veronica," he said patronizingly. "You can use it."

"Wait a second!" It was Mark again, and he was obviously upset about something. "I don't believe this. Somebody swiped the hood ornament from my car!"

Dan suddenly leaped out of the way as Veronica floored the gas pedal. As the car screeched forward Allegra had just enough time to pull item twelve out of her purse and wave it triumphantly under Mark's nose.

"Bye, Mark!" she called. "You can have it back on Monday night—after we win!"

*   *   *

"Table for three, please." The maître d' looked wearily at Allegra and her party and shook his head.

"What's the matter, Pierre?" Allegra asked. "You look a little frazzled since yesterday."

Pierre stifled a sigh. "Table for three?" he repeated, obviously controlling his impatience. "Fine, fine, right this way."

Sabrina touched Allegra's shoulder. "What's his problem?"

Allegra shrugged, and the three of them were led to a table near the back of the room.

"Crowded tonight, isn't it?" Allegra asked conversationally, but Pierre merely gave her an exasperated look and turned to leave. "Pierre?" Allegra pressed. He turned back with a smoldering look. "May we have menus right away, please?"

"Menus?" he asked. He gestured grandly around the room. "Why do you need a menu? Do you see anyone else asking for a menu? *Non.* Of course not. And do you know why?"

They all shook their heads, wildly curious, but Allegra's face dropped as she followed his gaze around the room. "Oh, no," she whispered. "They're all here."

"Who?" Sabrina started to ask, but her face froze as she followed Allegra's eyes.

"Oh, no." Veronica groaned. "The entire Mangia Society is here." Sure enough, the restaurant was filled with the participants in the scavenger hunt. Each table was occupied by groups of either men or women. Allegra caught Carla's eye and returned the thumbs-up sign her friend showed.

"You want the trout mousse appetizer, correct?" Pierre

asked. They nodded dumbly and he stalked off, mumbling something in French under his breath.

"This is crazy!" Allegra said flatly, looking around at all the familiar faces. "They can't *all* be here."

"Why not?" Mishi called over from the next table. "It's the first item on the list. Besides, this restaurant is closed on Sunday and Monday. It's our only chance."

"But why everyone?" she persisted. "Only one member of each team has to—" She stopped abruptly as she saw Dan and Colin and Mark enter the room. It didn't take long for them to see what was going on, and their faces lit up with broad grins. Mark caught Allegra's eye immediately and smiled wickedly. She turned away, trying in vain to ignore him, but he strolled right over to her table and looked down at her. His presence was so magnetic that Allegra would have felt ridiculous maintaining an air of indifference. With a tiny sigh, she looked up to meet his eyes, which, as she feared, sparkled with a shrewd blend of amusement and challenge.

"You're too late," she said at last. "We got the last table."

"Then you won't mind if we join you," he said. It was a statement, not a question, and Allegra felt justifiably annoyed. They were supposed to be on competing teams. He couldn't just waltz over and demand access. It wasn't fair.

"As a matter of fact, I do mind," she said coolly, congratulating herself on her poise. "And besides, I don't see why all of you have to be here just to get one item." She looked around the crowded room. "This is insane. We've all got to split up and get more organized."

"She's right," Sal said. "But what the heck—I thought it would be fun to come here. So what if more than one guy gets this mousse stuff?"

"Not the mousse," Allegra pointed out. "The recipe. And take it from me, it's not so easy to get."

"We know that," Sal said patiently. "We tried. But we thought that if we could all taste it, we'd figure it out."

"This is ridiculous," Allegra insisted. "I'm an expert, and I'm not sure I can do it." She stood up and appealed to the entire group. "Have you all tried the mousse?" Several heads nodded. "And has anyone figured out the recipe?"

No one answered. They were all too busy eating.

"Listen, everyone," she said authoritatively. "We can't overrun a restaurant like this. It's bad public relations for the Mangia Society. Besides, there are too many other items to get, and we've got to be more coordinated. I think the subteams should get busy tracking down their portions of the list."

"She's right," Sal said suddenly, consulting the next few items. He stood up and addressed them. "We can't all go trooping into the Rare Records Room at the library or invade the maternity floor at New York Hospital." He turned to his colleagues. "Let's go."

"Okay," Carla agreed, throwing down her napkin. "Mitzi and I will take items nine through fourteen."

Little by little, items on the list were reassigned and papers flew back and forth as agreements were made. The contest was fueled with new enthusiasm as everyone rushed out of the restaurant. Allegra watched the mass exodus in amazement. After ten minutes, only a few people were left, and she, Veronica, and Sabrina remained alone at their table. Even Mark had somehow disappeared during the confusion, and neither he nor Dan nor Colin were anywhere to be seen.

"Where's Dan?" Veronica asked suspiciously.

"I was just wondering that myself," Sabrina said. She

looked around the empty room, and suddenly her face lit up. "I'll bet they're in the kitchen!" she exclaimed.

"And I'll bet you're right," Allegra said, jumping up and heading toward the kitchen. "Leave this to me."

She got no further than the service station at the back. Pierre was frantically trying to arrange a dozen plates of trout mousse. "Oh, no!" she said at once.

"What now, mademoiselle?" he asked, clearly peeved. "Do not rush me, I implore you. The other orders will be ready soon. Michel is making another batch especially for this crazy group."

She groaned and stepped around him, tiptoeing fearfully into the kitchen, where a chaotic scene met her eyes. Michel was mixing a mysterious blend of ingredients in a huge blender and behind him, three assistants were hastily cleaning fresh trout. The chef looked up and saw her, greeting her with a suspicious "Humph."

It was a delicate time to try and get the recipe, but Allegra had an instinctual feeling that it was now or never. The ingredients were right in front of her, if only she could get the proportions. She took a bold step forward, trying to summon the tact she would need to wheedle the information out of Michel, but he was too busy to even notice her. In the back of the large kitchen, a delivery man dressed in a white uniform took inventory as two other men unloaded large sacks of onions and potatoes. Everyone there was busily intent on doing something and no one had time to indulge her curiosity. She was about to swallow her request and go back to inform Pierre that he could forget about the rest of the orders, but Michel mumbled something to himself that seemed to be directed at her. Finally he looked up at her, one finger in the air.

"The answer is still no!" he announced, thoroughly

provoked. "It was no yesterday afternoon, and it is no tonight. And if you will excuse me, mademoiselle, I have an order for thirty more of the mousse."

"I'm not going to tell him," Allegra mumbled, backing away. She was about to give up and shrink out of sight, but something near the back caught her eye. Another delivery man had replaced the first, but he turned away and hid his face as he scribbled furiously onto a pad. There was something strangely familiar about him and Allegra marched right through the kitchen and confronted him, tapping him pointedly on the shoulder.

"Uh—yes?" When he didn't turn around, her suspicions were confirmed.

Refusing to be deterred, she walked around and stood in front of him, looking accusingly into Mark's guilty but triumphant face. Silence passed between them, as each stared at the other.

"Well, hi," he said at last, surreptitiously tucking the pad into his pocket.

"What do you think you're doing?" Allegra asked, her eyes narrowing.

Taking her firmly by the arm, Mark led her quickly out of the kitchen and into an alcove. She trotted along with him, casting a helpless look back at Michel, who was too busy to notice them. "What were you writing down?" she asked in a loud whisper.

He smiled confidently. "Nothing that concerns you. Don't worry, it's all under control. I think we should be getting along now, don't you?"

She reached boldly into his pocket searching around for the note pad.

"Hey!" he exclaimed, his fingers locking around her wrist. "What are you doing?"

"I want that recipe!" she fumed, still trying to reach for it.

"Well, you can't have it," he said coolly, easily keeping her at bay. "We're on opposing teams, remember?"

Allegra stopped her struggle and stared at him. "Why, you hypocrite! You didn't think so before, when you wanted to sit at our table."

"All's fair in love and war." He shrugged.

Allegra realized that she was dealing with a man who would stop at nothing to get what he wanted. He would try any trick in the book, and if it didn't work, he would try another one without batting an eye. She would have to fight fire with fire.

"You know what your problem is?" she asked teasingly. "You spend too much time fraternizing with the enemy."

He lifted an eyebrow, but before he could respond, she looped her arms around his neck. "Come on, Mark. Give in." The feel of him so near and so vital sent a shock through her that she hadn't anticipated. Mark had a clean, masculine scent, and his golden-brown eyes raked deliberately over her face. Allegra hesitated for only an instant, and then she gathered her courage and kissed him gently on the mouth. The kiss was piercingly sweet, startling both of them for a second. Allegra was about to back down in confusion, but Mark's powerful arms encircled her and drew her close. The kiss deepened immediately as his tongue found its way into her mouth, and then they were both lost in a whirlwind of sensation that tasted of honey and promise. Allegra could scarcely remember why she had initiated this contact. The moment their lips met, she had forgotten everything but how wonderful it was to lose herself in his arms. The electricity between them was so intense that it assaulted her every time it became physical. There was no reason, no logic—only an unbearably sweet tide of desire washing over them, uniting them on the same current.

Mark's hands slipped up her back and traced dizzy lines on her neck and shoulders. His fingers played luxuriously with the wild thickness of her hair and then dropped down to feel the feminine curve of her wrist, settling finally on the swell of her hips. His mouth lifted from hers only to seek the sensitive skin of her throat, where he left a trail of kisses that made her tingle in response.

Only after Allegra had let out a tremulous sigh did Mark stop, satisfied that he had aroused her as much as he had wanted to. Allegra thought she felt his hands trembling on her hips, but perhaps she was the one who was trembling. She opened her eyes hastily and they focused on the breast pocket of his jacket. Without thinking, she lifted one hand and reached inside.

"Nice try, Allegra," Mark said, grabbing her hand and holding it in a viselike grip. "Did you think you could melt my defenses with one mere kiss?" She gave a little cry of frustration and her eyes flashed, but he wouldn't let go of her hand. "I'm afraid you'd have to distract me with far more than a kiss in a hallway," he continued huskily.

Allegra did not want to hear the insinuations that were likely to follow. Her blood was still racing, and she needed to stand back and let her head clear so that she could think rationally. Standing so close to Mark Trackman put her under a crazy spell that enchanted her as much as it controlled her.

"I must confess," he continued in the same dark tone, "I'm wildly curious as to what your body looks like under that dress. If it's as beautiful as it promises to be, we could be in for a very interesting evening of exchanges."

Allegra pulled her hand free with one fierce yank and used it to push him rudely away. "How dare you talk to me like that?" she snapped.

Mark sighed. "You disappoint me," he said calmly. "After all, you're the one who threw yourself at me. I was merely responding. Besides," he added with a slow smile, "I want to prove to you that there are many things about women that I like very much indeed."

"I can see that," she answered, trying to sound sarcastic and failing miserably. Why had she kissed him like that? She had wanted a way to get the recipe, but she wouldn't have kissed just anyone to get it. She had to admit to herself that she wanted to kiss *him*.

Mark watched the tumble of emotions on her face, and his tone softened. "Please don't feel embarrassed. I always enjoy it when women throw themselves at me. Of course, I don't always respond. But you were more than convincing." A look of pure pleasure crossed his face as he remembered their kiss, and he stepped forward, taking her in his arms again. She expected him to kiss her with an obvious sense of possession, as the winner of an argument gloating over his victory, but their embrace was nothing like that. As soon as Mark touched her, the same, inexplicable magic slipped between them, lifting them up to a plane that had nothing at all to do with arguments or contests or control. He didn't kiss her but merely looked down at her with such tenderness that Allegra thought she would melt then and there. Mark Trackman, always so sure of himself, always so strong and breezy and unemotional, was searching her face with an intensity that thrilled and yet frightened her. A moment ago she had wanted to be rid of him. Now she would be happy to stand there in his arms for the next century, if no one interrupted them.

But someone did. The maître d' rushed frantically by on his way into the kitchen but stopped in his tracks when he saw them standing there. He took one look at Mark in the white uniform and frowned.

"Is something wrong, Pierre?" Allegra asked, trying to step nonchalantly out of Mark's arms. She faced him brightly, not wanting to reveal her jumble of thoughts.

But Pierre was not concerned with her. His gaze lingered sternly on Mark. "Monsieur," he said. "What are you doing here in that uniform? Deliveries are in the kitchen."

Mark gave him an enigmatic smile. "Leaving," he answered. Without another word, he strolled out into the dining room and disappeared.

Allegra stood rooted to the spot, too surprised to move. She turned helplessly to Pierre, hoping he would somehow understand, but he was standing with his arms folded, a haughty expression on his ruddy face.

"This," he said, handing her a small slip of paper, "is for you."

She looked down at it and back up at him. "What's this?"

"Your bill," he said with a pompous air. "For thirty-six orders of trout mousse." He grinned. *"Bon appetit."*

"I still want that recipe, Trackman." Allegra said an hour later as they stood in front of the Gotham Men's Club. Mark leaned against the front of his car, wishfully fingering the spot where the hood ornament was supposed to be.

"I knew I'd run into you here," he said matter-of-factly.

Allegra shrugged. "Where else would we look for item seven?"

A sudden commotion echoed from inside the building, and Mark ran to the door. "Ready to go, guys?" he called.

There was no answer.

"Fellows?"

"Do you know I had to pay for thirty-six trout mousses?" Allegra asked.

He turned. "I'm sorry to hear that," he said, but he couldn't hide the smirk that crossed his face.

"Over a hundred bucks," she added, hoping to make an impression, but Mark wasn't interested.

"The moon will be full tomorrow night," he informed her. "That means bears." He looked at her carefully to see if she understood.

"Bears?" she repeated. "What do you mean, bears?"

He smiled wickedly and strolled back to his car. "Why do you think they call it Bear Mountain?"

Dan and Colin came running out of the building before she could think of a fitting reply. "It's gone!" Dan said dramatically.

Mark stood up eagerly. "It can't be gone. Are you sure you looked in the right place?"

"Of course," Colin answered impatiently. "Someone beat us to it."

Mark shook his head adamantly. "That is impossible. No one has the key except me."

A small tinkling sound made them all look up. Allegra dangled a set of keys from one hand and gave them all a cool smile. "You forgot the back way," she said to Mark. "I use it for deliveries."

A station wagon came roaring up to the curb at that moment, and Veronica leaned out the window. "Let's get going," she said to Allegra. "This thing is falling halfway out the back."

Allegra ran to the back of the station wagon and winced at the sight of the huge, stuffed black bear that had been squeezed inside. Its head protruded out the back end, its white teeth exposed in a weird, timeless grin that seemed to mock her.

"Very funny," she mumbled to the bear.

Mark laughed. "Between the bears and the slugs," he said baitingly, "you'll have your hands full tomorrow night."

Allegra gulped, but Veronica beckoned hurriedly. "Come on," she said. "The night is young. We still have time to get a few more items." She smiled sweetly at her husband. "How are you fellows doing? Get the bear yet?"

Allegra tried bravely to climb into the back of the car. The bear took up most of the space, and it wasn't easy maneuvering around it. Allegra also had the uneasy feeling that the bear would somehow come alive and say something to her. It was spooky to be riding around in the moonlight, squashed next to an imposing bear that had once been very much alive.

Veronica wasn't interested in her friend's predicament. She drove away in a flourish of exhaust fumes and a roaring engine, honking to be sure that the men would stay out of her way. As they sped down the street, Allegra looked back at the three of them standing under a lamp post. Mark watched the car as it sped away, a broad smile on his face, and Allegra realized in a flash that he admired the group's ingenuity. They had smuggled the bear right out of his precious club, and he knew it. Although Allegra didn't want Mark to know that she was looking at him, he lifted an arm and waved in an oddly congenial manner before she turned away. Well, that was nice of him, she thought as she started to automatically wave back, but her hand went straight into the claws of the bear and she winced in pain.

"Ow!" she said, and sighed.

"You okay back there?" Sabrina asked.

"I think so. Lions and tigers and bears. Oh, my!" They all laughed as the car turned and headed downtown.

The next hour and a half was filled with mounting excitement and growing confidence as they found item after item on the list. By midnight, the station wagon was loaded not only with the bear, but with an infant's T-shirt stamped with the words "New York Hospital," a street sight that read DON'T EVEN *THINK* OF PARKING HERE, an empty bottle of Jax beer that they had bought at a theatrical supply store (the extinct New Orleans brand was often used in productions of *A Streetcar Named Desire*), a clown suit, and the top half of a mannequin from Bloomingdale's. The mannequin had been surprisingly easy to get. Sabrina had once designed windows at the large department store, and the guard still remembered her. She had convinced him to let her borrow the necessary item, promising to return it on Monday. The mannequin had a male head and was not clothed in anything except a tag around its neck.

Holding the mannequin in place, Allegra firmly placed an arm around it and sat squashed between the bear and all the other items. Broadway was crowded with traffic as they bounced along but Veronica was like a driven woman, intent on finding just a few more items before they called it quits for the night, so she drove mercilessly through the maze of cars, buses, taxis, and pedestrians.

"Slow down!" Allegra called. "I'm going to get killed back here!"

"Take it easy," Veronica assured her. "Everything's under control." At that moment, the car hit a pothole, and the back end of the station wagon was sent jouncing out of control into the air. Everything they had collected rattled noisily out of place and then fell down again. Everything appeared to be intact, except the bear, which had flown right out the back window. It lay in a massive heap in the middle of Broadway with one paw extended dramatically as if imploring aid.

Brakes screeched and horns blared as irate drivers were forced to a halt in the middle of the street. "Hey, lady!" a voice called. "Get that thing outa here!"

Veronica scrambled out of the car and ran around to the back, where she began tugging frantically at the bear. Sabrina got out and helped her, trying to lug the heavy animal into the back of the station wagon. They were so busy that they didn't notice Allegra, who was lying on her back, pinned helplessly underneath the mannequin.

"Help!" she cried indignantly, but the noise from the growing swell of traffic drowned her voice.

"Can you reach over and grab a paw?" Sabrina asked. "The least you can do is help."

"Help?" Allegra repeated impatiently. "This dummy landed on top of me when you jerked to a halt, and the street sign is on top of the dummy."

Sabrina gasped as she perceived Allegra's plight, and she managed to push the sign away as the cacophony around them intensified.

"Oh, no!" they heard Veronica gasp. "Look who's here!"

"Who?" Allegra asked, still pinned under the mannequin. "I really can't imagine."

"Well take a guess."

"I don't know, Prince Charles?"

Mark Trackman stuck his head inside and looked quickly around the disheveled car. He caught sight of Allegra and immediately feigned embarrassment. "Oh, excuse me," he said deferentially. "I didn't know you were with someone."

"Don't be ridiculous!" Allegra tried to push the mannequin away once more, but its arm kept swinging back over her chest.

"What an ardent admirer," Mark observed. "He can't keep his hands off you." He lifted the dummy with one strong movement and pulled Allegra out of the car.

She looked around at the traffic jam and moaned. Dan busily directed the cars around them, and Colin helped Sabrina load the bear back into the car.

"We figured you weren't far behind us," Mark noted. "The stage manager at the Booth Theater said you had just left—"

"With the original 1936 playbill from *You Can't Take It with You*," Allegra finished for him, holding up a small, framed item. Mark took it and examined it with interest. "I must say, I'm impressed," he said. "How did you ever get them to part with it?" He eyed her suspiciously. "Or do they even know you have it?"

"They know, all right," Allegra answered proudly.

"Of course they do," Sabrina added self-righteously. She and Colin were still pushing the bear's hind legs into the car. "I had to leave them a deposit check."

Colin blanched. "For how much?"

"A thousand dollars," she said airily.

Colin gulped. "Well, take good care of it," he admonished.

Allegra took the framed playbill firmly out of Mark's

hands. "Let me have that," she said. "You can look at it another time. Right now, I don't trust you."

Mark laughed. "Now, now. This is a gentlemen's game. We'll have no stealing or cheating."

"Are you a gentleman?" Allegra asked him warily.

"Of course."

"Well, I'm not." She grinned. "So watch out!"

A loud blast from a horn made them all jump. A patrol car was in back of them, its red light sending flashing beacons across the busy street. "Let's go, folks," a policeman said through his loudspeaker. "You're holding up traffic." The patrol car pulled up next to the station wagon, and the officer shined his flashlight inside. "Look at all that junk," they heard him say to his partner.

"We're almost finished," Veronica explained smoothly. "We lost something that fell out of the back." The policemen looked at the bear and raised their eyebrows, but they didn't seem all that surprised. Anything was possible on Broadway in the middle of the night, and they had seen it all.

They managed to squeeze the bear back inside, and Allegra stared doubtfully at the station wagon. "I don't think I'm going to be able to fit in there anymore," she said. "Maybe I should grab a taxi and call it quits for tonight."

"So should we," Dan said to Veronica. "It's late." He looked imploringly at his wife. "Would you mind giving me a ride home?" They lived on Long Island, an hour away.

Veronica pretended to think about it, but finally grinned. "Sure, why not?" she quipped. "We'll call a truce for tonight."

"I won't touch any of your loot," he promised. "Scout's

honor." He got in and turned to Sabrina and Colin. "Can we give you a lift?"

Colin eyed the paraphernalia in the back nervously. "Uh—no, thanks," he said. "I don't think we could all fit inside."

Veronica winked at Sabrina and Allegra. "See you both tomorrow," she said. "At Bear Mountain." They all waved as she drove off.

Colin and Sabrina said goodnight and strolled up Broadway, deciding to walk home in the balmy night. Allegra and Mark were left standing in the middle of the street.

"I've got my car," he reminded her after a pause. "Can I drop you off? I'll take you anywhere you want to go."

"I doubt that very much," Allegra said dryly, pointing to where he had left his car double-parked. A tow truck was raising the front end of the sleek vehicle, preparing to tow it away. Mark took one look at the truck and let out a yell that was heard by everyone on Broadway.

"Wait a minute!" he called, running over to his car. "What are you doing?"

"You were double-parked, buddy," the city employee replied matter-of-factly. He continued with his work, deftly positioning the truck.

"But—but that's my car!" Mark wailed.

The uniformed man didn't bother to answer as he raised the front end of the car. Mark winced as a clanking sound emanated from inside his car. All the items that the men had gathered on the scavenger hunt were packed inside, and as the car was upended, everything fell backward, one on top of the other. Mark and Allegra jumped as a sudden crash sounded.

"I hope that wasn't the gallon of Elmer's glue," Allegra said, repressing a laugh.

"Look," Mark protested, trying to reason with the man in the truck, "I was only double-parked for a second. We got stuck here, and—" Another crash made him groan elaborately as he slapped his hand to his forehead. "That," he announced mournfully, "was the glue."

Allegra stepped forward, unable to resist her own curiosity, and looked into the backseat. A stream of white liquid steadily streamed out of its container, covering everything else in sight. She looked at Mark, who had turned away, his face in his hands.

"My car," he was moaning to himself. "My car!"

Allegra patted his arm sympathetically. "Don't worry," she said. "You can pick it up tomorrow." She looked again into the backseat and brightened. "Say, where did you get another bear's head? I didn't think you'd find one. It's—oh, no."

"What?" he asked in a choking voice without turning around. "Go on, tell me."

"Well, the bear now has glue all over its head."

"Oh, my God!"

Allegra laughed softly, and Mark shot her an accusing glance. "Well, it's only a car," she insisted. "I'm sure it can all be cleaned off somehow."

"You don't understand," he muttered darkly.

"Yes, I do. You are in love with your car. Typical masculine possessiveness. I can't believe how upset you are."

The car was secured with a final, agonizing jolt. "What a mess," Allegra observed wryly. "I have to admit, you fellows got a lot of things we didn't know where to find. I can see the Chinese mask and the beer keg." She stole a peek at Mark. "Now they'll all be glued together for easy carrying."

Mark snapped at that last remark and ran over to look inside his car. He froze when he saw the mess. "What a disaster," he said, approaching the driver of the truck with grim determination. "Please, Mister," he said, "just let me get inside and clean it up at least."

"Sorry, Mac," the man said apathetically. "I got a job to do. You were double-parked and holdin' up traffic."

"But surely there must be something I can do to—"

"No, there ain't, Mac. Sorry. You can pick her up tomorrow over at the lot. It'll cost you a hundred bucks in cash, plus forty for the parking ticket, of course." He shifted into gear and prepared to pull out.

"Cash?" Mark repeated nervously. He pulled out his wallet and leafed quickly through his billfold. "But I don't have that much on me in cash—and the banks are closed until Monday!"

"Then they'll see you on Monday!" the driver retorted.

Mark stepped in front of the truck and tried a new approach. "I demand that you listen to reason! Just let me look inside for a moment. Is that too much to ask?" He looked disheveled and crazy standing there in the street barring the path of a tow truck. Allegra realized that only Mark Trackman could become so impassioned about a mere machine.

"Oh, come on, Mark," she said soothingly. "Don't get crazy over this. Talk to the man nicely. Maybe that will work."

Mark looked at her with a gleam of hope. "I didn't mean to be rude," he said to the driver with chilling politeness.

"No problem, Mac. I get it all the time."

Mark smiled painfully. "Then you'll be so kind as to release my car?"

"Negative, Mac. Let's get moving."

Mark looked at Allegra as if everything was all her

fault. "Polite didn't work," he shouted. "You got any better ideas?"

"Forget it," the driver yelled out the window. "Nothing works. There are a million lines, and I've heard them all."

The driver lurched menacingly out of the space, causing Mark to jump out of his way. Standing next to Allegra, he watched as the sleek Alfa Romeo was unceremoniously carted off.

"What you need," she announced firmly, "is a drink."

"What I need"—he sighed grimly—"is not to get mixed up with flighty women who need to prove that they are just as good as men."

Allegra turned to him angrily. "That was uncalled for!"

He shrugged. "You may be right. But thanks to you, this whole scavenger hunt business has caused my car to be smothered with glue and towed away."

"And you had nothing to do with it yourself?" she demanded. "You're the one who goes stomping all over the world on ridiculous adventures. In your heart of hearts, you're Rama of the Jungle!"

"And who are you?" he shot back. "Calamity Jane?"

Allegra burst out laughing. "Maybe I am," she admitted with sudden compliance. The whole ordeal now seemed so very funny. Not only were they chasing all over town in pursuit of ridiculous items, but Mark's car had been drowned in glue and towed away. Allegra continued to roar with laughter as cars whizzed by, and her cheeks grew rosy as she pointed at Mark. "Don't be so pompous about it," she gasped, in between peals of laughter. "You really fell apart watching your gorgeous car being towed."

His mouth turned up on one side. "I love that car," he said.

"You're like a little boy who had his favorite toy taken away from him," she remarked, and burst into fresh laughter.

"You're really enjoying yourself, aren't you?" he asked dryly.

"Oh, yes. Aren't you?"

"Well . . ." His eyes narrowed in fun, and Allegra knew she had won. Suddenly Mark began to chuckle too, and this time Allegra was the object of his mirth. "I thought I would keel over when I walked into the party tonight and saw you standing there with one guy under each arm. You looked like Tugboat Annie!" He threw his head back and roared, and Allegra had the good grace to laugh along with him. "And when you were stuck underneath that mannequin!" He laughed until all the tension and aggravation slipped away, and when he stopped, they faced each other with new awareness.

"How do you feel now?" Allegra asked softly.

"Much better." He thought. "And hungry. Are you hungry?"

She nodded. "I'm starved. I didn't eat anything at the party." There was a pause as the obvious possibility of their eating together hung between them. "Listen," Allegra said at last. "I'm really sorry about leaving you in that elevator yesterday. I shouldn't have done it. Let me take you out for dinner to make up for it."

Mark considered. "I must say, an offer from the president of the Mangia Society is tempting. But I have an even better idea. Why don't you make dinner yourself? Let me sample your cooking and see if I like it."

Allegra laughed. "All right," she agreed. "It's very late, but what the—" She stopped abruptly as she realized something. "My purse!" she cried. "I left it in the station wagon!"

"So you'll get it tomorrow."

"But my keys are in there! Now I can't get into my apartment!"

Mark took her arm and the warmth of his touch was amazingly comforting. "Follow me," he said with an air of mystery. "I'll put you up for the night, and I promise you'll like it."

"Your apartment?" she asked suspiciously, but Mark shook his head.

"No. Someplace better." He gave her a smile so full of charm that Allegra almost melted then and there. "Trust me."

Oddly enough, she did.

Chapter Five

❦

The Seventy-ninth Street Boat Basin was nestled on the West Side of Manhattan, right next to the Hudson River. Allegra had noticed it from time to time when she happened to be driving by, but she had never seen it up close, nor had she ever had reason to go there. As she and Mark pulled up in a taxi, their arms loaded with the food they had purchased on the way, she grew strangely quiet.

"Is this where you're taking me?" she asked in a low voice.

He nodded. "This is it. Last stop."

"You have a boat here?" she guessed. He nodded again, and she smiled almost wistfully.

"What is it?" he asked quickly.

"This whole area seems . . . distant," she answered after a pause, looking around. "I know I'm still in New York, but suddenly it feels like a whole new world."

He grinned thoughtfully. "I know what you mean." They stepped out and stopped for a moment, savoring the peace and quiet as the cab drove off. Mark led her silently down a flight of stone steps to the embankment, and when they rounded the stone wall, a beautiful and utterly calming sight met her eyes.

Long piers crowded with boats of every description lined the old wharf. The pleasant lapping of the water contrasted gently with the occasional squeak of pulleys and the flapping of ropes. The clear white moonlight shone over everything, lending a definitive, if ethereal, air to the site.

"Another world," Mark said. His voice was pitched very low, as if he did not want to disturb the harmony of the scene.

Allegra did not answer. The frustrations of the day magically disappeared as she stared out over the water, and suddenly Mark Trackman was no longer the attractive but annoying man she had been battling for two years. He moved differently down here, with surprising lightness and grace, and he walked along the dock almost stealthily, like a cat with its tail high in the air. Allegra followed him wide-eyed, reluctant to break the silence.

At last he stopped in front of an enormous white hull that was majestically silhouetted against the blackness of the river. "This yacht is yours?" she whispered. He nodded quickly, completely at home in this unearthly setting. Allegra's eyes followed the ghostly shadow of the boat, and she carefully made out the name that was etched onto the side: *Trailblazer*. "It's so big," she said in awe.

"Seventy-eight feet," he explained briefly. "My father took it all over the world." He jumped nimbly onto the deck. "I'd like to take her around the world someday myself," he added after a moment. "But somehow . . ." He trailed off, and Allegra sensed that there was something about this topic that bothered him. She could scarcely believe she was here with him, in this lovely, silent place. Here he was inviting her on board a boat in the Hudson River, confiding in her, and letting her see one of the places that he obviously loved best.

She took a deep breath of the cool air and sighed.

"That sounds wonderful," she said. "To go around the world on a boat."

He looked up and smiled. "It's just a dream."

She was startled and secretly flattered. A dream? Mark Trackman was sharing his dreams with her? She shook her head as if to dislodge the fantasy, but the shadowy boat and the quick-footed man remained resolutely in her line of vision.

"Well," she said at last, "let me know if you ever need company. I'd be more than happy to oblige." She said it offhandedly, and instantly wondered if she had said the wrong thing. But Mark didn't seem to mind at all.

"Want to come along?" he asked.

Allegra covered with a laugh. "Just call me when you're ready to hoist anchor."

He smiled and loaded the food they had brought onto the boat. Allegra was still standing on the dock, and he reached out a hand to help her aboard. She stepped onto the old, smooth wood and was instantly aware of the gentle rocking motion of the boat. Their hands were still locked, and they remained that way for a second longer than was necessary. She knew that something was going to happen between them, and she didn't want to think about or analyze the situation for too long, for fear of destroying it. She would let the inevitable take its course.

Mark seemed to know it too. His eyes were charged with a brightness that Allegra had never seen before, but perhaps it was only the moonlight. Anything seemed possible in this peaceful setting.

"Come on," he said in the same hushed voice.

She followed him down a few steps and found herself in a hallway that was longer than her whole apartment. Mark led her through the first door and into a large, fully equipped kitchen. It was larger than her office kitchen, she noted with a grimace. She wondered how much he used it, and her eyes traveled curiously over the many shelves, cupboards, and utensils that hung from hooks on the ceiling.

Wandering through a gracefully rounded arch, she found herself in a dining room filled with the elegance of another era. Eight portholes on each side let diagonal slants of moonlight shine into the room, and a large crystal chandelier hung majestically from the ceiling. An oval mahogany table stood in the center of the room surrounded by upholstered Queen Anne chairs. Carefully detailed wainscoting framed all the walls, giving the room a harmonious look. As Allegra stared at everything, she could hear the persistent lapping of the water and the occasional cry of a lone bird.

"Are we still on for dinner?" Mark asked, coming up behind her. "Everything you might need is here. I'm always well stocked."

Allegra turned to face him, and a long, silent moment passed between them. Mark's face was a mask that she could not read, and she sensed that he was not yet ready to take the next step with her. She almost smiled as she realized that although Mark knew all about survival and adventure, Sabrina had been right about one thing: sometimes men needed to be handled with care.

"What would you like?" she asked softly. "How about a soufflé?"

She watched as one tawny eyebrow lifted. "A soufflé? We don't need anything that fancy, do we?"

She smiled. "It's not that fancy. It's just a puffed-up omelete. Do you like asparagus?"

He held up a hand. "Surprise me then. I want to see what the head of the infamous Mangia Society can do in a kitchen."

"Okay. Watch."

He did, and in the next several minutes Allegra whipped together a blend of eggs, asparagus, and a simple base that turned into a fluffy concoction. She poured it all into a baking dish and popped it into the oven. "Wait until you see how it comes out," she said.

She stopped talking, realizing that she was making normal conversation with him. They had always found plenty to say to each other in the past, even though most of it had been antagonistic. Now that the antagonism had vanished, they were suddenly at a loss for words, and each felt rather shy. Allegra took a long, deep breath, relishing the anticipation that was building. She couldn't be sure exactly how the evening would end, but she did know that nothing would ever be the same between them after tonight.

They walked out of the kitchen and into the dining room, stopping in front of the portholes. Outside, the Hudson River looked inky black, and they could see the pinpoints of light on the opposite shore. Although they were docked in one of the world's most frenetic beehives of activity, they were calmly poised on a vessel that could easily take them out into the open sea, to foreign ports and unseen lands.

"Do you really want to go around the world on this boat?" Allegra asked.

He hesitated. "Why not? Who wouldn't want to? It's just that . . . well, I'm not sure it's the right time. I wouldn't want to be disappointed."

Allegra was puzzled, but she said nothing. She suspected that there was more to Mark's answer than he was letting on, but she knew better than to press the issue. The delicate balance that hung between them was slowly strengthening, and she would do nothing to upset it.

"Would you like a glass of wine?" he asked.

"I'd love some," she said.

He went back in the kitchen and returned a moment later with two crystal goblets, a bottle of red wine, and a corkscrew. Allegra examined the bottle and couldn't hide her surprise.

"Chateau Latour, seventy-two!" she exclaimed. "Are you sure you want to open this?"

"Why not?" he asked mildly.

"Do you drink wine like this all the time?"

He grinned and shook his head. "No. But I'm in a festive mood tonight for some reason." He wound the corkscrew into the bottle and carefully pulled out the cork, which made a soft, popping sound that spoke gently of pleasant things to come. Mark poured wine into the two glasses and handed her one. "Cheers," he said.

"Cheers." They clinked glasses wordlessly and sipped, savoring the full-bodied, mellow flavor of the excellent wine. "This is wonderful," she said after a few more sips.

"Would you like to see the rest of the interior?" he asked.

She nodded eagerly and followed him into the hallway, where he stopped in front of a framed oil painting. It depicted a group of early-twentieth-century men on horseback. "The founders of the Gotham Men's Club," he explained.

Allegra examined all of the faces, trying to determine which man was Mark's ancestor. She deliberated, chose, and pointed. "Your great-grandfather?" she guessed.

He nodded, surprised. "Right you are. Does he look like me?"

"No," she admitted, "but he has the same I-can-do-anything-I-want look about him." She swallowed, wondering if she had said too much, but Mark was unperturbed.

"Thank you," he said graciously. "I take that as a compliment."

She continued on down the long hall, stopping to admire another picture, this one a yellowed photograph from the First World War. "Who's this?" she asked curiously.

"Can't you tell?" She stared at the young man in the picture, but it looked like no one she knew. "That's Wendell," he informed her.

"Wendell!" She took another, closer look. "You're kidding! How old is he?"

He smiled in a way that was somehow proud. "Close to ninety."

Now she was even more surprised. "Ninety!" she repeated. "I thought he was in his seventies."

"He's one of the lucky ones," Mark said in a clipped tone. "Let me show you something." He led her into a smaller room that held a cracked leather armchair and a gleaming, imposing rolltop desk. Allegra admired its beauty, but Mark was fishing avidly in the drawers for something. He pulled out an old album and handed it to her.

"Look at this," he said. His tone was more of a command than a request, but Allegra was used to this attitude already. Curiosity compelled her to do as he said.

She opened the album and examined the aged photographs. They were interesting but did not give her a clue as to why he wanted her to see them. As she slowly turned the pages, revealing a diploma, a marriage license dated 1919, several more photos, newspaper clippings, and yellowed letters, she realized that she was looking at the summary of one man's lifetime. A *London Times* article dated August 11, 1922, covered a safari he had led in Africa. Another one had a picture of the man standing next to a caged tiger in front of a mountain range.

"Who is this man?" she asked. She carefully read his name aloud. "Marcus Willoughby."

"My grandfather," he said. "On my mother's side."

"What a life," she said reverently. "I'm impressed. Where is he now?"

Mark's mouth tightened as if he didn't want to talk about it, but he answered readily. "Right here in New York. I was able to get him into a home near the club. The Medicaid people wanted to ship him upstate, but I managed to get him a place here in town." He shook his head grimly. "Those people can be awfully hardheaded, but I don't take no for an answer when it comes to something like this. They didn't want him to leave the damn place, not even to come over to the club three times a week, but Wendell found a special bus service that picks him up. They take him—" He stopped, disconcerted by the look on her face. "What is it?"

"Nothing," she said quickly, looking down. "It's nice that you were able to do this for him." She knew that he would be embarrassed if she said more, but the truth was that she found it more than merely nice. Mark was revealing a side of himself that perhaps no one ever saw. Certainly she had never suspected that such tender concern existed under his polished exterior. Allegra looked at him curiously, wondering what other secrets he held tightly. "You're full of surprises," she said quietly.

"Why? Because I take responsibility for things? I don't need any laurels for that." He put the album back in the desk without further comment, and Allegra's respect for him went up another ten notches. Not many people would take that kind of responsibility in stride. She looked around the room in awe.

"Who's that?" she asked, pointing to another painting.

"That? Oh, that's old Clipper. He was in the club yesterday when you walked in."

"And I suppose he has all kinds of great achievements to his credit?" she asked.

"Well, he went on an expedition to Antarctica and was the only man to come back in one piece. There are extensive files at the club if you want to read all about it." He stopped short, realizing what he had just said. "Uh, I mean I could take them out and show them to you, if you're really interested." He coughed and turned away, and Allegra hid a smile. She had made much more of a dent than she had realized.

He led her back into the hall, past more framed photographs and documents, but the room they had just left continued to stick in her mind. The Gotham Men's Club was apparently more than an old relic. It was an old-age home of sorts. What kind of world did Mark live in? Was he so surrounded by history that he was unaware of the present?

And yet he was so stalwart in the role he had assumed. No one had asked him to do it, but he had accepted the responsibility of the Gotham Men's Club's survival. Indeed, he had personally seen to it that the elderly members were safely cared for. The whole operation seemed to rest entirely on his shoulders. Allegra found the sense of history and continuity extraordinary.

Mark led her through a maze of rooms, all of which were large, comfortable, and well appointed. She had never seen anything like it before. Standing in the middle of the enormous reception room, Allegra impulsively threw her arms out and spun around in a circle. "I don't believe this place!" she cried, throwing her head back and letting her lush hair fly freely around her face. Mark stood to one side and watched her, his face changing with the shadows her movements cast upon it. "I can't get over all this space!" she continued, whirling over to the portholes that glinted with rays of moonlight. Her face glowed, and her eyes shone like two dark jewels set in her face. She stopped and looked at Mark standing motionless by the door. His body was silhouetted starkly in the doorframe, one elbow leaning against the wood. It was impossible to ignore the radiant masculinity emanating from him, and the fact that he seemed unaware of its power made it all the more magnetic. A shiver went through her as she watched him shift his weight from one lean leg to the other.

"Let's get back upstairs," he said huskily.

Allegra nodded breathlessly. "The soufflé should be just about ready," she said. She glanced at the ornate clock on the wall and saw that it was almost one-thirty in the morning. Somehow, she didn't feel tired at all.

Back in the kitchen, the pleasant aroma of the soufflé gently permeated everything, and Allegra smiled as she took it out of the oven. It was golden brown and puffy, having risen successfully to a full three inches over the rim of the dish. She put it on the counter and quickly found plates and forks.

"We have to eat it right away," she explained as she pierced the crust with a spoon and began to dish out the light, fluffy mixture. "If we don't, it will collapse."

Mark watched her appreciatively. "You're not very patient, are you?" he asked suddenly, but his tone was teasing rather than abrasive.

"No," she admitted, "not very." She handed him a

plate and smiled. "A soufflé is one thing that just can't wait."

"But some things are worth waiting for."

She handed him the other plate. "Like what?"

"Like waiting for the right time and place. Like waiting to change your life." He spoke seriously, inviting a thoughtful response.

"Do you want to change your life, Mark?" she asked gently.

"Do you?" He set the plates down at the small oak table in the kitchen and poured two more glasses of wine. They sat down and looked at each other across the table.

"Cheers," he said, lifting his glass.

"Cheers," she whispered. They drank, their eyes locking, and Allegra was potently aware of the unspoken questions and answers hovering between them.

Mark tried the soufflé. "Mmmm!" he said at once, nodding vigorously. "This is great! You're right, it's kind of like a puffed-up omelet with asparagus in it."

The soufflé was creamy in the center, practically melting in their mouths. It disappeared quickly, as did the robust wine which added sparkle to their eyes. It was finished in a matter of minutes, and suddenly Allegra felt shy. "I—I really should try to call Veronica," she said. "I don't have my keys . . ."

Her voice died away as Mark reached across the table and took her hand. She felt the slight shock of it, and then the irresistible warmth. "Don't worry about that," he said softly. "You'll get them tomorrow."

"But I have to get my camping equipment," she said weakly, knowing somehow that he would have a way to take care of that problem too. He did.

"Don't worry about that either," he said with a little smile. His fingers tightened around hers. "I have loads of equipment right here on the boat. You can borrow a tent if you like, and I have several pairs of fatigues. I even have hiking boots in several different sizes stashed away in one of the bedrooms. This boat has been around for a long time, you know. It's collected a lot of junk."

Allegra nodded, but she was barely aware of what he was saying. The obvious question of where she would spend the night loomed before her, but she didn't have the nerve to bring it up. She was sure he would have an answer, and it wasn't necessarily one she was ready to hear. He was making it all so easy, perhaps too easy. Mark Trackman was the sort of man who knew how to get what he wanted, and if he had suddenly decided that he wanted an enchanted evening with her, he was certainly making it happen. But what else had he decided? And with what strings attached? Allegra looked up, feeling more decisive than she had all evening.

"Mark," she said, reluctant to break the spell but knowing she would never forgive herself if she didn't find out what she needed to know. "Why did you bring me here?"

His eyes, which had unraveled her so many times before, met hers, but this time there was a candor in them that she had never noticed before. "I thought we were calling a truce, Allegra. I'm tired of playing cat-and-mouse games. Aren't you?"

That was a good beginning, but it wasn't enough. "But everything seems to be going your way," she said. "I'm still out in the cold as far as the Gotham Men's Club is concerned."

"What do you mean?" Mark asked, clearly surprised. "I thought we had that settled. The winner of the scavenger hunt determines the outcome. If you win, you get that space. And if I win," he added, the familiarly confident grin lighting up his face, "the club gets a year of Saturday night dinners, courtesy of the Mangia Society."

"You mean to say you're serious about that bet?" Allegra demanded.

"You mean to say you're not?" His voice challenged her, and Allegra knew that he wasn't going to let her back down.

"It's not really fair," she insisted. "Renting that space is something I should be able to get anyway. But a year's worth of free dinners . . . you're going to break me, Trackman."

He grinned. "You agreed. Don't tell me you're going to welsh on your bet."

She threw down her napkin. "All right, all right. You win."

"Not yet. But soon." His hand was still holding hers, imprisoning her fingers in its warmth. The tone of the conversation was teasing and shaded with the old banter they had engaged in before, but it had definitely lost some of its former edge. The antagonism seemed remote, and it now seemed completely natural that they were holding hands. Suddenly Allegra realized how natural it would feel to do more than hold Mark's hand.

A slow, contented smile spread across her rosy face. Mark's eyes traveled over her features with a lean, hungry expression. "Do you know what you look like right now?" he asked huskily. She shook her head, her dark eyes wide. "You look like an earth goddess bearing ripe fruits, fragrant grains, and sweet blossoms."

Allegra could think of absolutely nothing to say. It seemed impossible that Mark Trackman had just said such words to her, and yet his voice fell on her ears as easily as silk. A tremor passed through her body, and his eyes suddenly filled with desire. "Do you know what I'd like?" he continued in the same tone.

"What?" she whispered breathlessly.

"I would like to make very slow, delicious love to you. All night long." His eyes never left hers, and she felt her heartbeat take a perilous jump. "I think we've been headed toward it, but we didn't want to see it. Because once we cross that barrier, Allegra, there won't be any turning back. You know that, don't you?"

She looked down, but she nodded slowly.

"Then come." He stood up, taking her with him. She trembled as Mark tenderly ran his hands through her thick, wavy hair, lifting it sensuously and letting it drop again to her sloping shoulders. "I want to see you," he murmured. "All of you. Every inch. Do you have any idea how long I've wondered what your body looks like underneath those floaty little dresses you wear?" His hands caressed her shoulders and slid down her bare arms, making her tingle. "I've caught glimpses of you going in and out of the building, and I've always found myself staring at you." Allegra closed her eyes for an instant, but she opened them again just as quickly. His face was mesmerizing in the moonlight. Lined with desire, the tawny eyes smoldered with intensity, and the patrician lines on his brow moved and flickered in the shadows. "Tell me you want me," he said. "Tell me."

His hands circled her waist and firmly traced the contours of her hips.

"I do," she whispered raggedly. "I do want you. I should have known it before. But I couldn't . . ."

The fire that crackled through him at her words seemed to flow right through his fingertips and into her body. A deep, fevered well of passion rose within her, one that she knew would soon be out of control.

"What were we afraid of?" he wondered aloud, his hands still roaming over her body.

"We weren't afraid," she answered brokenly, reaching up to touch the hard, flat lines of his chest. "Just stubborn."

"Yes," he agreed. "You were a royal pain in the neck."

"And so were you," she answered with the last ounce of control she could muster. They laughed together softly.

Her head was thrown back and her lips were parted in mute invitation. Mark gazed down at her for one final, endless moment before gathering her close and kissing her with all the longing that had built up between them for so long. At first Allegra felt an explosion of the senses, like a vibrant display of firecrackers suddenly set off inside of her. The exhilaration of knowing what was finally happening drowned out every other reaction. But almost instantly the sweet desire coiled within her rose up to claim her, winding its tendrils around every inch of her. She became completely sensitive to his touch, fluttering in response wherever his fingers grazed. Her breasts seemed to expand, rising up to crush against his chest. He was instantly aware of Allegra's sensuality, and his heart raged within. Their tongues intertwined with liquid fire, transporting them to a realm that was above the confines of earth. Allegra was astounded at the depth of their responses. After only one heady kiss, she was ready to follow him willingly, wherever he sought to take her.

Together they walked down the long hall, hands clasped tightly, and Mark opened a door at the far end. Neither one of them spoke, but there was no need for words. The magic that was to come would speak volumes; mere words could only pale in comparison.

They walked inside, and Allegra quickly took in the brass bed visible through the streaks of moonlight filtering in through the row of portholes. Mark's arms held her again, his hands pressing against the soft, bare skin of her back. He kissed her once, very briefly, and then slowly lowered the straps of her dress without once taking his eyes from hers. Allegra felt like a goddess as his eyes fell to her supple throat and lingered at her full breasts, which gently swelled over her dress. His face was fired with a wonderful combination of desire and awe.

Mark drew her dress down several more inches, easing it over her lush breasts the sight of which he savored for a long, tantalizing minute. The dress slid down to her waist and he pushed it over her rounded hips, letting it fall to the floor.

Kneeling, Mark hooked his fingers around the elastic band encircling her bikini panties, and he gently pulled them down her legs. Allegra stepped out of them quickly and stood motionless before him, letting him drink in the sight of her body. Sitting back on the bed, Mark's keen eyes raked her naked form with raw pleasure. She stood there for several long moments bearing his scrutiny until at last he stretched out a hand.

"Come to me," he whispered.

She walked the short distance to the bed, her breasts bobbing slowly with her movements. Stopping in front of him, she stared down with sensual abandon into his open, passionate face.

"It's not possible," he murmured, molding his hands around her hips and tracing firm paths to the soft flesh around her back. "You are even more beautiful than I imagined."

Allegra gave a short cry and fell forward, gliding her body onto his. Mark gasped before throwing his arms around her and pulling her closely. They rolled over together so that Allegra was beneath him. He kissed her hungrily, letting his hands roam freely over every inch of her.

After several lingering kisses that sent them both into a whirlpool of sensation, Mark stood up and quickly shed his own clothes. The elegant attire disappeared, leaving only the tanned, athletic form underneath. Allegra stared at him just as he had stared at her, and he stood proudly, his feet planted apart on the floor. "I said I would make love to you all night long," he said. "And I will."

He joined her again on the bed, stretching his long, lean body out next to hers and leaning on one elbow. With one hand he traced long, dizzying lines and circles around her breasts, down her stomach, between her soft thighs, and up her smooth back. "You have a beautiful body," he proclaimed, taking one round breast firmly in his hand. "How can you manage to be slender and yet so voluptuous, supple, round, and yielding all at the same time?" Allegra could not give him an answer, in fact she could not talk at all. Her eyes fluttered as she tried to watch Mark's movements, but his hands were working a magic that reduced her to a pool of intoxicating desire. A long, silken "Ohhh" escaped her parted lips, and he smiled knowingly as he bent his head. Her moan changed to a sharp cry as he gathered her breast in his hand and took its rosy peak into his mouth. Feeding gently on her sweetness, he drew a response from her that was rooted deep within her. Her head moved wildly from side to side, her hair entangling within itself against the clean white sheets.

Mark now followed the trail his hands had created with the warm insistence of his mouth. He kissed her neck, leaving sensitive circles with his tongue, he savored the fullness of each sloping breast, he buried his mouth in the gentle swell of her belly, and he opened her legs to taste the soft sweetness of the insides of her thighs. Allegra was constantly aware of his innate strength, but he never used it to bend her to his will. His masculine prowess lay present but idle, preferring to be stated rather than proclaimed. He was exquisitely gentle, seeking and finding the most sensitive, secret parts of her body and patiently arousing them until she lay trembling helplessly on the bed.

Her hand reached out almost blindly and touched a solid wall of muscled chest. She exulted in its firm, hard lines, and explored further, discovering his taut, narrow hips and powerful legs. Mark lay back and reveled in her caresses, his hand reaching up occasionally to fondle a heavy breast.

"Allegra," he whispered, when she had tormented him as much as he had tormented her. "I need to have you. Now."

She held out her arms and he clasped her to him. The shock of his strong body against her soft, rounded form made her gasp in anticipation. She settled herself beneath him, holding him close and letting her legs open, but Mark propped himself up on his elbows and shook his head.

"No," he whispered raggedly. "I want to look at you. I have to see you." He adjusted his body so that he was lying directly next to her, and she instinctively threw a leg over his thighs and arched her hips.

With one hand, she reached down to guide him into her, and she touched a ready shaft of silken strength as it lodged against her body. They looked into each other's eyes, and they were very much aware of the transition that was about to be completed. Allegra's eyes closed luxuriously as he entered her, her body closing in around him, but Mark kept on looking at her flushed, dewy face as long as he could.

"Beautiful," he murmured softly as he sank deeply inside of her.

"So good," she breathed, savoring the feel of him inside her.

Then the slow spiral began, changing shape and color as they persistently climbed it. The newness turned into a smooth, fluid cadence, which then became sparked with tiny arrows of pleasure flying faster and faster until they reached a higher plane consisting no longer of the two of them, but of a unified presence.

"Look at me," Mark breathed hoarsely, and she opened her eyes to see his face. The face that had once been so controlled and taunting was now driven with passion, both fierce and gentle as he continued his sure, even thrusts. He studied her, taking in her dark eyes, smoldering with response, her oval face with its high color and smooth cheekbones, her parted lips, and the tumble of black hair that was spread out in glorious disarray.

Again the rhythm changed, this time to a high, feverish pitch that had only one destination. Suddenly charged with a single bolt of electricity between them, they opened the last barrier and flung together out of control. Allegra cried out, her hands gripping his arms, her breasts rising into a final peak of passion.

They floated slowly back to earth, sinking into each other's arms as the wild, savage colors gradually shifted into muted pastels. Allegra's head rested on his shoulder, nestling snugly into the contour, and at that moment she felt utterly at peace with the whole world.

At last her eyes opened, and the first thing she saw was the completely satisfied expression on Mark's face. Yesterday this man had been her adversary; tonight he was her lover.

Mark smiled to himself and held her closer. She kissed his shoulder and he opened his eyes lazily, drawing the covers over their shoulders.

"Are you cold?" she whispered.

"No."

"It's very late." The commonplace words had nothing to do with her feelings, and yet they seemed to augment the comfortable mood. She smiled mischievously. "Are you tired?"

"Mmmm." Mark rolled over, pinning her beneath him. His sudden burst of energy took her by surprise. "I am a man of my word."

Her fingers intertwined in his thick, sandy hair. "Are you?"

"Yes. And I intend to keep my promise." His strong arms slid underneath her body. "I said I would make love to you all night long, and I will."

Allegra giggled. "Are you sure? I don't want to force you." She kissed his forehead and his nose.

His mouth found hers and they kissed leisurely. "My dear Allegra," he said in the old, mocking tone she knew so well. "We've only just begun."

Chapter Six

It couldn't have been the unfamiliar hum that awoke Allegra in the morning, because its low, mellow vibrations seemed to have lulled her to sleep. And the gentle, persistent rocking of the *Trailblazer* had only added to the most restful sleep she had experienced in years. It must have been the relentless sensation of a forward motion that caused her to wake. Finally she opened her eyes once and for all and focused them out the porthole. It was open, revealing a patch of bright blue sky, and a delightfully cool breeze bathed her in fresh air. Beyond the water loomed the sheer, towering walls of the Palisades. It didn't make sense. Where were the buildings on the Jersey shore? The Palisades were way up the river. For several moments Allegra pondered this question, until finally the realization hit her that they were traveling up the river.

"We're moving!" she said aloud, turning to the empty space in the bed where Mark should have been. Of course he wasn't there, she reasoned, hitting her head with her hand. Someone had to be steering the boat. She climbed quickly out of bed and looked around for something to wear, not wanting to change back into her dress from the night before. Rummaging in the closet, she came up with an enormous sweat shirt stamped with a picture of a chicken. Under the artwork were the words "Arnie's Country Chicken." She slipped the sweat shirt and nothing else over her head and ventured into the hall, relishing the feel of the polished wooden floors beneath her bare feet.

Through the row of portholes she saw the George Washington Bridge, spanning the river with majestic grace under a cloudless sky. Allegra's spirits rose to buoyant heights as she climbed the steps and found her way to the steering room at the very top of the vessel. Mark was seated behind the large wooden wheel, pushing the throttle forward as she approached. His eyes focused keenly on the water, and she could tell that he hadn't noticed her presence.

Sneaking up behind him, she threw her hands over his eyes and said, "Guess who?"

Mark jumped a little, but he kept his cool and answered, "Elizabeth Taylor? No, no don't tell me . . . I've got it! Bo Derek!"

She jerked her hands away, but he caught them, turned around, and kissed her. "You are delicious," he pronounced. He sat back and took a long look at her. "Hi," he added softly.

"Hi." She grinned.

"We'll be at Bear Mountain State Park in a little over two hours," he informed her. "So we'll be just in time to meet the others at the base of the trail." Turning back to the wheel, he pressed forward on the throttle again, and she could feel the boat picking up speed. "Just listen to those engines purr," he said like a kid enjoying an expensive toy.

"I can't believe it," she murmured, stepping forward to look out at the water that parted smoothly just ahead of them. "I feel shanghaied."

"Hey, I left my car in the clutches of the city for this. I'll have to get it tomorrow. You don't want to miss the second part of the hunt, do you?"

She shook her head adamantly. "No way."

The boat settled into its new speed, and Mark turned once again. This time he noticed what she was wearing. "Good Lord." He laughed. "Where did you find that old thing?"

"In your closet."

"*My* closet? Well, it must be an antique." He grinned. "I hope you didn't choose it because it's self-descriptive."

She glanced down at the words "Arnie's Country Chicken." "Well, if I'm a chicken," she said tartly, "then you're a fowl."

"Ouch. Listen, there's a whole supply of clothing on this boat. You can pick out whatever you like."

"Later. In the meantime, how about breakfast? We can both use a hearty meal before we face off on the playing field."

"Good idea." He nodded. "You're the chef. I make my passengers sing for their supper."

"Get ready for the breakfast of your life," she promised.

In the kitchen, measuring flour into a bowl in order to makes crepes, she reflected on how much she had learned about Mark Trackman in an amazingly short time. After two years of renting office space from him, Allegra had never seen more than his most superficial side. She tried to remember all the times they must have ridden down in the elevator together, and how many times had she passed him in the lobby or bid a mechanical goodnight as she left for the day? How many times had she tried to call him to complain about something that wasn't working? And how many more times had she harangued him for neglecting to fix it? She shook her head wryly as she realized just how long she had been suppressing her magnetic attraction to him. Allegra had always assumed that he could not possibly be appealing to her. They were so very different in attitude and outlook. He was the mainstay of that stuffy old club next door that still barred women in this day and age, and she was the epitome of the modern, successful woman. Mark was exactly the sort of man she had always firmly believed should be severely let alone. An irrepressible giggle escaped her as she contemplated her present circumstances. So much for her snooty resolve! The night she had spent in Mark Trackman's arms had been a sensual and emotional experience that she would never forget. Her body still tingled as she remembered it.

Not that she had him figured out. He was still an enigma in many ways. She had never dreamed how well he took care of those elderly men in the club. Without his discreet attentions, most of them would probably have been shipped off to old-age homes by now. He had never referred to it, never indicated in any way the depth of his involvement. She had always thought he was merely a more youthful version of a bunch of stalwart has-beens.

She was so caught up in her thoughts that the first crepe was burning in the pan before she even noticed it. Smoke curled ominously from the skillet, and she hastily turned off the heat and ran cold water over the pan. Allegra couldn't believe what she'd done. Any novice could cook a crepe in a pan. She hadn't made a foolish mistake like this in years.

"Hey!" Mark called down from the upper level. "What's burning?"

"Nothing!" she called back. "Just a crepe."

"What?" he yelled.

"A crepe!" she called at the top of her lungs. "I burned a crepe!"

Suddenly a face appeared upside down outside the kitchen porthole. "Did I hear you correctly?" Mark demanded. "You burned something again? Last night it was the quiche. Now it's—"

She picked up a spatula and held it over his head. "If you tell anyone—"

"Tell them what? That the head of the Mangia Society can't cook? I ought to blackmail you for life."

"Go steer the boat!" she ordered. His face vanished as quickly as it had appeared,

Once again she marveled at how fast things had changed for them. The banter between them was now light and easy and no longer sparked with tiny barbs. As she rinsed the pan and poured in more batter, she felt that everything was somehow falling into place. Mark was still a puzzle, but she found the puzzle intriguing more than baffling. The pieces of the jigsaw were slowly fitting together, and she knew that before long all of them would be neatly in place. Her heart swelled as she thought of Mark masterfully steering the boat above. The warm sensation struck a deep, familiar chord in her, and the shock of its recognition was so strong that Allegra almost burned another crepe. Was she falling in love with Mark Trackman? She couldn't be. Not now. Not after all the times she had thoroughly denounced him. What would her friends say? They would never let her live it down. She sighed and took a firm hold on herself, deftly flipping the crepe in the pan. If she was going to indulge in shamelessly sentimental feelings, then she would keep them to herself.

Twenty minutes later, Allegra made her way back to the steering room, balancing a silver tray as she climbed the steps. Pleasant aromas emanated from beneath the silver covers, and Allegra reflected wryly that she hadn't found a single piece of stainless steel in the whole kitchen.

Mark was perched on a chair behind the wheel, lazily guiding the *Trailblazer* with his feet. His hands were laced behind his head, and the fresh breeze blew through the cabin like the promise of summer's fullness. He watched her approach with an appreciative grin. "Whatever you've got there, if smells great," he said encouragingly.

Allegra set out plates and forks and glasses, and then lifted the silver covers to reveal strawberry crepes, poached eggs, cinammon toast, and fresh-squeezed orange juice. Mark surveyed the feast with unconcealed admiration. "You really are a whiz," he commented, shaking his head. Allegra sat across from him and picked up a fork.

"Dig in," she said. "See if I earned my keep."

"You've already earned it," he said, taking her hand for a moment. His touch was warm and dry and he withdrew his hand reluctantly. "You know, I meant to ask you," he continued comfortably, as if they had been talking this amiably for years. "About those newsletters you mail out every two weeks. I found one of them in the lobby the other day. I must say, it wasn't anything like I expected."

Allegra's curiosity jumped. "What did you expect?"

"Well," he hedged, and then threw caution to the winds. "I thought it would be an amateurish collection of tidbits and recipes, like something out of a teen gossip rag. But I was very pleasantly surprised."

Allegra found, to her surprise, that she was very eager to hear his evaluation of her work. She put her fork down and waited as he took a sip of orange juice.

"You're a one-woman operation, aren't you?" he asked.

"For the most part." She nodded. "Except for occasional outside help for big projects."

"It's very impressive," he said. "I'm a magazine publisher myself, you know, so I know what I'm talking about. I noticed that you have advertisers from all over the country."

"And a circulation of over a hundred thousand," she added proudly, but she was unprepared for his reaction. His face dropped and he regarded her with a new look of respect.

"No wonder you want to expand," he said, nodding thoughtfully.

"Now you see why I need that space in the Gotham Men's Club," she added hopefully.

But he didn't take the bait. "I'm sure there are other alternatives," he said.

Allegra dropped the subject. The day was too beautiful in too many ways to have any kind of argument. Settling back in her chair, she looked out on the river where Sunday boaters slowly appeared around them. Sailboats, canoes, and even rowboats glided in the water while children already played with pails and shovels along the banks. They ate in silence for a few more minutes, and then Allegra cleared up as Mark returned to the wheel.

Back in the kitchen, Allegra washed everything she had used. The kitchen was extremely well stocked. If she had been expecting to find sides of beef and dreary rows of canned goods, she couldn't have been more wrong. The sophistication of the food Mark kept on hand led her to believe that he had been teasing her about being a Neanderthal type when it came to food.

Finding a large apron and tying it securely around her waist, she hummed a tune and began to prepare enough food for the camping trip. She was sure Mark wouldn't mind. She was in her element now as she quickly mixed and stirred, rolled and sautéed and browned. As the yacht made its way upstream and the mountains in the distance grew larger, she carefully wrapped up her preparations in several plastic containers.

"How are you doing down there?" Mark called down to her.

Allegra glanced at the clock. Over an hour and a half had gone by! "Just fine!" she called back, a trifle guilty that she had been so long in the kitchen. But the results of her efforts would make it all worth it. "Are we almost there?"

"A few more minutes. Why don't you go and find yourself some clothes? Second room on the left, lower level."

Allegra did as he suggested, opening the door to a room that was obviously used as one big closet. She hunted curiously through drawers until she came up with a loose pair of khaki hunting fatigues that covered her well enough, a sensible pair of sturdy socks, an old-fashioned safari hat that perched neatly on top of her curls, and a pair of hiking boots that were only a little too large. She thought for a moment and produced another pair of socks from the drawer. With the second pair added to the first, the boots fit snugly over her feet. They looked a little out-sized on her medium frame, but at least they were sturdy and comfortable. Modeling her new outfit in front of a full-length mirror, she giggled at her reflection.

"Very sexy," she pronounced. "It's a good thing Wendell didn't plan a beauty contest to top off the day's events."

She marched back up to the steering room and twirled

gracefully in front of Mark. "How do I look?" she asked with a coy smile.

"Well," he said dubiously, eyeing her bouncing breasts that were free beneath the khaki shirt. "It's an interesting advertisement for underwear." A sly twinkle stole into his eyes.

"I was wearing a dress with tiny straps last night, remember?" She shrugged.

"I remember."

She ducked her head. Neither one of them was likely to forget anything about the previous night.

In a few minutes, the boat rounded a bend, and they pulled up alongside a dock. Mark tied up the *Trailblazer* while Allegra packed everything she would take with her into a backpack. By the time Mark had his backpack ready, Allegra was fresh with excitement, ready for the contest ahead. He quickly strapped his own pack onto his back and then helped her on with hers.

"That's funny," he muttered. "Yours feels awfully heavy. What on earth have you got in there?"

"Oh, just a change of clothes, a sleeping bag, and some food." She looked puzzled, not knowing how she could possibly have packed any less.

"Food?" he asked suspiciously. "What kind of food?" His face changed with understanding. "You don't mean *real* food, do you?"

"Is there any other kind?" she floundered.

He laughed uproariously, and she returned his mirth with a stern frown. "You idiot!" he said merrily. "What did you do, cook up a storm and take it all with you?" She nodded, dumbfounded. "What are you expecting, an army?"

"Well, what are we supposed to do, starve?"

He laughed again and slipped off his backpack. Deftly

opening it, he showed her the contents. Allegra stared in disbelief as she examined dried packets of soup, freeze-dried coffee, powdered milk, potato flakes, and even a freeze-dried spaghetti dinner.

"That's how it's done," he said loftily. "And it all weighs less than half a pound." He lifted the pack easily and slung it back onto his shoulders. "That's how you pack for a two-hour hike up a mountain. I can see," he added with a confident smile, "that this contest is going to be even easier than I thought."

"I don't care," she retorted. "That stuff is not fit for human consumption. What do you do, just add water and stir it? Sounds like feed for livestock."

"Suit yourself." He shrugged. "But don't blame me if you can't make it up the trail."

"Don't worry about me," she added quickly. "I'll be just fine. Anything is better than having to eat that—that dog food."

He took her by the shouders and looked down gently into her eyes, making her melt immediately. "Listen, Allegra," he said sincerely. "I'm telling you the truth. I really don't want you to have to kill yourself." He grinned. "You can lose just as easily without making it harder. Take some of the freeze-dried stuff along. It's not so bad." He went up on deck to secure the boat and check in with the local authorities, leaving her to examine little plastic packets of chocolate pudding and something called "powdered cheese food."

She followed him up on deck a few minutes later, her pack neatly strapped onto her back. He looked at her with an approving smile. "Now, isn't that better?"

"It's not bad at all." She nodded, adjusting one more strap around her waist. "The weight is distributed so that my legs are getting the brunt of it."

"That's how it's supposed to feel," he said. "The whole idea of backpacking is to distribute the weight to allow for fifteen to twenty miles of wilderness travel. And by the time you get up to the top of that mountain, that pack will feel twice as heavy, believe me."

Allegra swallowed hard but faced him gamely. "But so will yours, right?"

He laughed and nodded. "I have to admit," he said easily. "I haven't been out in the woods for a long time." He thought for a moment and ruefully shook his head. "A very long time."

"Good," she said brightly. "Then it should be an even match." They shook hands heartily and left the boat, heading for the meeting point at the base of the mountain.

Bear Mountain State Park covered hundreds of square miles of forest. At the base of the trail, winding up to the top of the mountain, was a large field of mowed grass with several picnic tables and charcoal grills next to a small lake. Allegra and Mark hiked over to this area through a small trail that led away from the river. After only a few minutes, she was more than aware of the weight pressing down on her hips, but she didn't want Mark to know that she was having any trouble. As surreptitiously as possible, she readjusted the straps and tried to shift the weight. The last thing she wanted was to fall behind during the hike, and by the time they reached the place where everyone had gathered, she knew she was in for a long haul.

"It looks like just about everyone beat us here," Mark said as Veronica saw them and waved. Sabrina looked up and saw them together, her eyes slanting into her characteristically impish smile.

"I wasn't sure you would make it," she said slyly. "I

tried to call you since early this morning, but all I got was the answering machine. Now I know why." Her green eyes appraised Mark coolly, and she took Allegra aside. "Where did you ever get that outfit?" she asked. "You look like a real pro."

Veronica was even more intuitive. "You look like you're about ready to drop," she observed carefully. "Didn't you get any sleep?" Sabrina's eyes crinkled again, and Allegra managed to keep a straight face as Mark marched over to say hello to Colin and Dan. Once again the group was instinctively dividing itself into two camps. The race was on again. Allegra watched with mounting dismay as Mark strode briskly across the grass, taking each step like a conqueror claiming the ground. As soon as he was out of earshot, she sank down with an exhausted sigh.

"Help me get this contraption off," she hissed to her friends, fidgeting to release the straps.

Sabrina pulled the pack off and it fell to the ground with a loud thud. "This thing weighs a ton," she exclaimed. "What are you carrying in here—a dead body?"

Allegra shrugged. "Just the essentials, that's all."

"And you expect to get up the mountain with this?" Sabrina shook her head, baffled by the mysteries of backpacking.

"Nice threads," Veronica commented dryly. "I haven't seen clothes like that since the late forties." She pulled at Allegra's voluminous pants and laughed. "In fact, these *are* from the forties."

"I got them from Mark," Allegra confided, causing her two friends to exchange a glance. "I think they make me look very adventurous, don't you?"

"Like an old Tarzan movie," Sabrina noted.

A polite voice intervened as Wendell approached them. He was dressed in neatly pressed fatigues along with an L. L. Bean jacket and hat. He eyed Allegra's clothes with astute approval. "Ah, my dear Miss Russo," he said, leaning forward on his cane. "You are dressed quite appropriately, I must say. You remind me of my first wife who accompanied me on a safari through the Congo."

Sabrina looked up, interested. "You took your wife on a safari?"

"Well, not exactly," he said wryly. "It was her safari, and I was invited to join it. We weren't married at the time, but by the end of that trip, I was proposing to her."

"How romantic," Veronica said. "She must have been something."

Wendell nodded nostalgically. "Oh, yes," he said, "she was something else."

"Well, well, well," a familiar nasal voice came through the crowd. "If it isn't the president of the Mangia Society dressed as Sheena of the Jungle."

Allegra sighed as Zeebo eyed her appraisingly. Nattily outfitted in a navy double-breasted sports coat and charcoal-gray slacks, he had obviously overdressed for the occasion. He handed a checklist to Wendell, who looked it over and nodded vigorously.

"Excellent, my boy," he said. "Simply marvelous." He turned sideways in an aside to Zeebo. "You placed the final object in its appropriate place?"

Zeebo smiled broadly. "It's exactly where you said to put it. Actually," he mused, "I was surprised to find how easy it was to drive right up to the top of the mountain."

"What's the matter, Zeebo?" Allegra asked. "You're not going on the hike?"

He shook his head with exaggerated patience. "Heavens no. I appointed myself as Wendell's assistant. Someone had to drive up the trail and place all those items, you know."

Allegra frowned. "But you're a member of the opposing team!" she objected. "How do we know we can trust you?"

Zeebo looked mildly offended, as if his honor had been called into question, and Wendell broke in soothingly. "Now, now," he said. "I needed someone to help me. I wasn't going on a hike at my age."

"No one will be going if we don't get started," Sabrina said pertly. She looked at her watch, surprised at how late it was. "Two o'clock. It will be sundown by the time we get up there."

Allegra looked down at her heavy pack and sighed. "Sundown," she repeated glumly.

Wendell lifted a brow as he caught Allegra's expression. "Wherever you are when the sun goes down is where you'll camp for the night." She swallowed hard and said nothing.

"Let's get started," Sabrina said again, with a cheeriness that made Allegra wince.

They all trooped over to where the group was assembled. Allegra trudged behind with a lackluster gait.

"Attention, everyone! Attention!" Wendell called them all together and began to explain the final rules. "The Appalachian Trail will take you all the way up," he cautioned them. "Don't try to stray from it. It's not necessary. Just follow the white markings painted on trees and rocks. For those of you who are camping overnight, remember that there is water at the summit, near the camping site. Please remember, the trail might look easy when you start, but if you should fail to reach the top before nightfall, you'll not find it at all until morning. It's impossible to navigate at night."

Everyone nodded soberly, and copies of the list appeared as the teams planned their strategies. "Happy hunting to all of you," Wendell finished. "We'll meet again in front of the club no later than ten o'clock tomorrow night. And one more thing," he insisted, holding up a hand to quiet them one last time. "Don't forget to bring enough water. There is none available until you reach the top!"

Mark caught Allegra's eye and he patted his canteen securely. As the group began moving toward the base of the trail, he found his way over to her.

"Have enough water?" he asked in a patronizing tone.

"Of course," she answered breezily. To prove it, she uncapped her canteen and took a long swallow. A slight hissing sound of escaping air and bubbles emanated from it, making Mark look up in curiosity. He grabbed it from her and took a sip, looking decidedly surprised at what he tasted.

"This is not water," he stated flatly.

"It's better," Allegra said smugly. "It's Perrier."

Chapter Seven

❧

"I found the first thing on the list!" Veronica called from way up ahead on the trail. Almost everyone had passed Allegra on the narrow trail, and only Mark had lagged behind to keep her company. The day was glorious, perfect for a mountain hike, and the cool breeze escalated pleasantly as they ascended the trail. It was the first real summer day of the season—the sun was warm, the leaves had burst into fullness on the trees, and the lush canopy of branches overhead provided dappled shadows along the path. The only sign of human intervention was the series of white markings on the trees, guiding them unerringly along the trail.

Allegra plunked down on a rock to rest for the third time in the first half hour, and Carla and Mitzi came up from behind. They could hear excited voices up ahead as Veronica examined her prize.

"What did she find?" Allegra called up to Dan, who was just disappearing around a bend.

He turned back and called down to her, "An arrowhead."

Allegra crossed that item off her copy of the list and reflected that this part of the hunt was going very differently from last night. Since there was only one narrow trail, they were all obliged to move together, and the obvious division between the two teams was much less intense. In fact, there was an overall feeling of camaraderie as husbands and wives hiked together just as if they had planned the outing themselves. It would have been much more pleasant if Allegra wasn't so disconcerted. It no longer felt like a contest, and she was already tired of lugging the backpack. The night she had spent with Mark was now far more interesting to her than the feud they had sparked. She wished privately that she could spend the day alone with Mark, cementing some of the discoveries they had only just begun to make.

Her reverie was interrupted by a short, startled scream. "That sounded like Sabrina," Mark said.

"She must have found the second item on the list," Allegra said with a laugh. She crossed off the item labeled "slug" on the list. There was another, more indignant scream, this one followed by a high series of giggles. "Yup." Allegra nodded calmly. "She found the slug."

Carla and Mitzi looked relieved. "I'm glad *I* didn't have to get one of those slimy things," Mitzi purred, brushing off the silk scarf she wore over her Calvin Klein active-wear ensemble. Allegra repressed a grin as she saw Mark look Mitzi up and down with barely concealed disapproval. The outfit was right out of a Bloomingdale's window, and it was completed by a pair of high-heeled designer boots that were obviously giving her trouble on the rocky trail.

"Well, that's two items down," Carla said jauntily. "We're doing very well." She and Mitzi sauntered on up the trail, leaving Mark and Allegra alone at the end of the straggly procession.

Allegra looked at him with a what-the-heck grin. "I guess we'd better get going," she said, wishing he would suggest going AWOL from the contest and spending the day alone together. "It's a good thing this is an endurance contest and not a race," she added wryly. "Or I'd definitely come in last."

Mark helped her up and tried to encourage her. "Come on," he said heartily. "It's not so bad. If you can climb up an elevator cable, you can make it to the top of Bear Mountain."

She hoisted herself up and began the slow plod once again, but after only ten minutes she was ready for another rest. The pack felt twice as heavy as it had when she had started out, and she was discovering muscles she hadn't known existed. The trail grew steeper, rockier, and narrower every minute. She expected Mark to be sympathetic, maybe even to emulate Wendell's everlasting courtesy, but he only grew more and more impatient with her inexplicable weakness. Allegra was in no shape to get into arguments with him. She pushed herself along, panting and sweating, until at last she undid the straps of the backpack and let it drop to the ground.

"Ugh!" she said. "I have had it! Endurance is just not my strong point."

Mark stopped and folded his arms, clearly annoyed. "You'll just have to force yourself," he said, tapping his foot against a stone. "None of the other women are having this problem. I don't see why you are."

Allegra plunked herself down on a rock and wiped her forehead, too exhausted to argue. Mark looked at his watch and pointed at it sternly. "Sundown is in less than two hours. At this rate we'll never make it." He took out his canteen and shook it. "I have just enough water left. Without water, no food. Don't forget, all we have is freeze-dried packets. So let's get moving."

He lifted her pack for her and his face changed angrily. "This thing is heavy as hell. No wonder you're so tired!

It must weigh four times as much as mine. What did you put in here?"

"Just some clothes, a sleeping bag, and food," she answered evasively, taking a sip from her canteen as Mark felt the outside of her pack.

"Food?" he asked suspiciously. "It feels more like a pair of dumbbells in there." He swung back onto the trail without looking back at her.

"Can't we rest just a few more minutes?" she pleaded. It was a rhetorical question. With a long sigh, she slung her pack on and trudged after him, wishing fervently that she had never tried to rent space in the Gotham Men's Club. The silence between them was definitely strained, and at last she told Mark to go on ahead. She would manage by herself. He started to object, looking remorseful that he had snapped at her, but she waved him on. "It's all right, Mark, really. I'd almost rather be alone for a while. I know I'm keeping you back."

He looked at her shrewdly and finally agreed. "Let me give you some encouragement," he said. "You can meet me later on." He took her into his arms and held her close, which wasn't easy considering that she was carrying a pack that felt like a pile of cannonballs on her back, but his mouth found hers with ease. They kissed with a brief, stinging intensity, and Allegra closed her eyes and savored the sweetness. She wished they would run off into the woods together like a pair of woodland spirits, but he had other ideas.

"This is still a contest," he reminded her lightly, flicking her chin with his hand. "And I still intend to win. After it's over, we'll talk about some new ground rules." He turned and strode ahead with such vigor and energy that Allegra's heart sank. This day was never going to end, and if it did, she knew she wasn't going to like the outcome. But there was nothing to do but go on. One foot after another, yard by yard and tree by tree— the trail became a blaze of monotony that was underlined by the heat of the sun and the exertion of the trip.

A thousand years went by as she trudged along, but at last she rounded a bend and encountered another human being. Sabrina was seated neatly on a rock, looking like an elf who had been caught unawares. "How're you doing?" she asked with piercing cheerfulness.

"How much farther?" was all Allegra could ask.

"Just follow the yellow brick road," Sabrina joked. She pointed into the forest. "That way. Everyone else is way ahead, but it's no longer uphill from here, so the walk is much easier."

"Why are you back here?" Allegra asked.

"I'm just resting for a while. Don't wait for me. I'll catch up in a minute." Sabrina smiled her impish smile and pointed again at the path, which looked smaller and denser as it wound into the trees. Allegra contemplated plunking down and joining her for a few minutes, but she knew that if she stopped now, she'd never leave the spot.

"Well, thanks a lot, scarecrow," she quipped, marching ahead. Sabrina looked puzzled. "*Wizard of Oz*," Allegra explained briefly as she left her friend behind. She considered going back and waiting again, but it was nice to know that she was no longer the very last person in the line. The pleasant thought of relating that to Mark drove her on, and before long she found herself deep in the heart of the forest, the trail barely visible. The white markings still existed, but the path no longer seemed to have any rhyme or reason to it. She took a turn and went further, lost in a maze of undergrowth that left no room at all in which to walk. She was alone on Bear Mountain, and suddenly she had the irrational fear that she was the only one there. She moved faster and faster, instinctively trying to reach human contact, and fear rose within her as her pack tugged mercilessly at her hips.

"Lions and tigers and bears," she muttered aloud, in an effort to lighten her mood, but it didn't work. The trees were so dense that the sunlight was nearly blocked out. She found herself in deep shadow as she struggled to find the path.

As long shadows began to cast themselves across the mountain, Allegra realized that she hadn't seen a white marker in quite some time. Her mind began to race as panic surfaced, closing her throat and making her heart race. I'm lost, she thought desperately. I must have taken a wrong turn and missed the trail.

She was too exhausted to go any further, and she dropped directly onto the nearest log to rest and catch her breath. It wasn't so bad, she reasoned. She had a sleeping bag and enough food. The weather report had predicted a clear, balmy evening. She even had some water left. This thought was particularly soothing, and she unzipped her pack to take out another bottle of Perrier. She unscrewed the cap and drank directly from the bottle, letting the cool liquid sink refreshingly into her tired body.

"Better not drink it all," a commanding voice said.

Allegra almost dropped the bottle as she whipped around, eager to see who else was there. Was it a member of the Mangia Society? Some derelict wandering in the woods? A forest ranger?

It wasn't any of those people. It was Mark, leaning casually against the side of a tree.

"Good Lord," she said, her body sagging with relief. "You scared me." She looked around ruefully and shook her head. "I think I took a wrong turn or something and got lost."

He answered matter-of-factly. "You *are* lost, and so am I." He let his pack slip to the ground and extended a hand toward the bottle of Perrier. "Mind if I have a sip? I'm all out of water."

She hesitated and then handed him the bottle. "Just this once," she admonished. "This is still a contest, remember? I'm not supposed to aid the enemy."

He gave her a don't-get-funny look and took a long swallow. "Okay, okay," he said, wiping his mouth. "I'm sorry I left you behind." His tone softened. "You know, I would have come back for you if you hadn't shown up."

She tried to smile at him, but she was too worried. "So, the great trailblazer himself is lost?"

"Yes," he admitted calmly, looking around as if trying to figure out where he had gone wrong. But he didn't look too worried. He looked more annoyed, as if the trail should have known better than to confuse them. Allegra's searching face caught Mark's attention, and he chuckled softly.

"What's so funny?" she demanded.

"I'm actually lost," he said. "And on Bear Mountain, of all places."

This confirmation of their predicament hardly cheered her up. "Oh, that's not macho enough for you?" she asked helplessly.

"I've been in all kinds of crazy places, some of them pretty dangerous. The Amazon, India, the Arctic Circle—the list is endless—and I've had all kinds of mishaps, but I've never actually been lost." He laughed again, aggravating her even further. "Don't you think it's ironic that an experienced explorer can't find the top of a mountain on a simple trail in a state park?" His peals of laughter echoed distantly in the trees, and Allegra shuffled uncomfortably.

"Well, it happens now and then," she said, not knowing if she was comforting him or reassuring herself. But at least he was here. She no longer had to face this wilderness by herself. She smiled, trying to look brave. "I guess we'd better go back the way we came and try to find the right path," she said sensibly.

Mark shook his head, dismissing the idea. "Too late now. The sun will be gone soon. We're better off right here." He pointed to a cliff rising in a clearing about fifty feet away. "That's a perfect place to pitch a tent and bed down," he said, his words sounding like an order. But Allegra wasn't ready to completely hand over the reins to Mark. Not yet, anyway. This was still a contest of sorts, and she wanted to make some of her own decisions. She reached into her pack and extracted a book she had found on Mark's boat. It was a guide to camping in the wilderness, and she turned at once to the section on choosing a campsite. Scanning quickly, she discovered that the area Mark had pointed to was right on target with what the book suggested.

"Sounds good," she said sunnily. "That's just where I was planning to pitch my tent."

Mark glanced back at her with a sly grin on his face as he marched off to the site and started pulling ropes, poles, and stakes out of his pack. Allegra continued thumbing through the book until she realized Mark was staring at her quizzically.

"Yes?" she asked. "Is there something on your mind?"

"Are you planning to pitch your own tent?" he asked bluntly.

"Well, of course," she answered, trying to sound more confident than she felt.

He frowned. "Don't you think that's unnecessary under the circumstances? After all, we're both lost. What can be gained by sleeping apart in two separate tents?" He walked over to her, his tawny eyes assessing her flushed, tired face. "Last night was just the beginning," he said softly.

Allegra was suddenly confused. She had wanted, even wished that Mark would feel this way on the trip, but now that he was saying so, she wasn't sure she should give in. This wasn't a pleasure trip, after all, but a contest. She was supposed to pitch her own tent and cook her own meals over a fire that she had built, and she wasn't going to cheat, even though she was alone with him in this remote setting. It somehow seemed important to remain sensible, especially now. Allegra had a vague feeling that Mark would never let her forget this expedition if she allowed him to take over.

"I—I don't think so, Mark," she said shakily, gathering her resolve. "The rules are very specific. I know it would be nice," she added hastily, wanting to kick herself for using such tame language. Last night had been far more than "nice." "I just think we should follow the rules, even though we're both stuck here," she finished lamely. She expected him to give her an argument or to try to persuade her to change her mind. A part of her even hoped that he would look suitably wounded and then pine away for her all night. But he merely nodded and went back to his side of the clearing, leaving Allegra feeling slightly deflated. Having made her decision, she would have to fend for herself.

While unloading her tent and all its equipment, Allegra stole glances at Mark in order to see what he was doing. He was obviously an experienced camper, and she noticed that he followed the instructions in the book to the letter. First he gathered firewood in the dwindling light, starting with a pile of small twigs and building up to larger branches. Then he arranged several large stones in a circle around a small pit he had dug and placed the small twigs inside the circle in the shape of a teepee. He added pieces of dried bark, and when she looked up again, he had a cozy fire burning in a matter of minutes. Allegra was impressed with the speed and skill he had shown. The next time she glanced at him, he was pounding the stakes around his tent into the ground and unrolling his sleeping bag. Mark pitched his tent so quickly that Allegra missed the finer points, and now it was her turn to follow suit.

"Looks easy enough," she muttered to herself. Closing her book, she gathered wood, imitating Mark's method of sorting twigs, kindling, and logs. She dropped everything into a neat pile and decided she had better see to the tent before it got too dark. The fire would have to wait. She stood back and glanced nervously at Mark to see if he had noticed. Although he looked off into the trees, she had the distinct feeling that his gaze shifted over to her as soon as her back was turned. She wasn't sure she wanted him to look at her because there was the possibility that she would make a complete fool of herself. When the tent lay in a heap in front of her, she regarded the folds of nylon and the stack of stakes and poles with dubious confidence. But as she examined the fabric and discovered the holes through which the stakes were meant to go, her spirits lifted and she set to work. The project almost faltered at one point when she realized she was setting up the tent inside out, but she quickly remedied the problem without mishap. The whole thing turned out to be so easy that she was humming a merry tune to herself by the time she pounded the last stake into the ground. Now she did want Mark to see her, and she stood back proudly to survey her handiwork.

"*Voilà*," she said loudly, opening her arms in a flamboyant gesture.

Mark threw her a cool glance. "Very nice," he commented dryly. He broke into a smile. "Not bad at all. I must say, you're living up to your own standards."

Allegra's confidence skyrocketed, and her enthusiasm for the scavenger hunt returned in full force. She could do anything Mark could do, and if she didn't know how, she was quite capable of figuring it out. "Thank you," she said in a spirited tone.

This was working out much better than she had anticipated. It was now time to see about dinner, and that was something she was always good at. As she bustled about, opening her pack and reaching for the food she had brought, Mark's voice came floating over to her.

"Would you be so kind as to allow me to use some of your water—I mean, Perrier?" he asked with deliberate politeness. "As you know, I am all out of water." He held up a packet of freeze-dried coffee and smiled.

She was about to acquiesce when she remembered that they were on opposing teams. She would have to stick to her guns. "Sorry, Mark," she said, "but no deal."

His face changed rapidly, and the polished courtesy vanished. "What do you mean, no deal? Aren't you hungry?"

"Of course I'm hungry"—she smiled—"but unfortunately, that's not going to help you much, is it?" She looked contentedly at her pile of wood and her beautifully pitched tent, secure in her competence. "Perhaps you had better start foraging for wild foods in the woods. I'm sure you must know a lot about that."

Mark stared at her with a very dark expression, but she ignored him with all the poise she could muster. She reached inside her pack and her eyes lit up in appreciation. "Ah," she said coolly, extracting a package of plump chicken breasts sautéed in sherry and lemon juice, "this should hit the spot." Mark's eyes widened as she continued to search in her pack, taking out a salad of pea pods and mushrooms, baked potatoes stuffed with black olives and gruyère cheese, a container of cream of watercress soup, and two fat apricot tarts. "Now there's just one thing more," she murmured, reaching into the bottom of the pack. "Oh, yes, here it is—trout mousee à la Michel—to go." She looked up brightly. "I paid for over thirty of these, you know. Might as well enjoy some of it." Her expression changed critically as she examined it. "Not quite fresh, I'm afraid, but under these circumstances, I don't suppose I can be picky."

"I don't believe it," Mark said finally, finding his voice. "You brought real food."

"Of course," she answered loftily, lifting out a bottle of wine. Mark almost choked when he saw it.

"That's a bottle of my best white wine," he protested, pointing.

"I know," she admitted calmly. "And I'll be happy to pay you for it if you like. For all of this." She gestured at the feast, since after all, it had come from his galley kitchen.

"Pay me?" he repeated in disbelief. "I don't want any money! I just want some food!"

"I know. But your freeze-dried potatoes should keep you happy."

Mark stood up and came over to her, sitting down next to her with a morose expression. "All right, Allegra," he said contritely. "You win. I was wrong. I apologize."

"Apology accepted."

"Good." He beamed. "Now where shall we start?"

" 'We?' " she said crushingly. "Forget it. I just

accepted your apology, that's all." She took out a small saucepan to heat the soup in and unwrapped the chicken breasts. The aroma of sherry and lemon rose gently to their hungry noses, and Mark fell back like a little boy sent to bed without supper.

"Do you realize what that smell is going to do?" he asked. "It's going to attract every animal in the forest." He paused to see if this would frighten her, but she remained unperturbed. He sighed. "What's for dessert?"

She pointed to the apricot tarts. They were a glazed golden pink in the dim light, and she smiled as she looked at the flaky dough. This was indeed a feast fit for a king. She had lugged it all the way up here, and now she was going to enjoy it. All she had to do was get that fire started, and she'd be all set. Once again ignoring Mark's scrutiny, she reached for her book on camping and turned to the appropriate chapter. She read for a moment, nodded intently, and set to work. Mark watched in astonishment as Allegra picked up a few shavings of birch bark and found a pointed stick. Holding the book in one hand and the stick in the other, she read aloud, " 'Turn the stick in your hand until the point becomes hot. Blow steadily on the shavings until they begin to spark.' " She put the book down. "Sounds easy enough."

Mark seemed to be holding back some kind of profound reaction. "Why not just use my method?" he asked.

"This *is* your method," she replied, turning the stick in the pile of shavings.

"If you had watched me," he insisted, "you would have seen that I used a very simple method—a lot simpler than this."

Allegra didn't believe him. She knew perfectly well

that this was his method, and she continued rotating the stick with hopeful determination.

"This is ridiculous," Mark stated after several minutes. "You can't—" He stopped abruptly as a tiny curl of smoke floated up from the shavings. Allegra bent over immediately, blowing gently and rhythmically until finally a few sparks appeared. She pushed the shavings and the twigs against the sparks, and suddenly, in a triumphant burst, a small but sturdy flame appeared. It spread rapidly to the surrounding sticks, and Allegra had a fire going.

"I did it!" she cried jubilantly. "I did it!" She scooped up another handful of twigs and threw them onto her fire, quickly following with a bunch of larger kindling. The fire crackled, and she quickly added a few fat logs. As the flames rose into the air, she spun around in a circle and threw her arms out exultantly. "I did it!" she cried again, as Mark looked at her in sheer admiration.

"You certainly did," he admitted after a moment. "I'm proud of you." Allegra sat down next to him, and he reached over and gave her a firm, lingering kiss. The kiss reminded her of just how much she wanted him, giving her instant doubts as to just how far she was willing to proceed with the stringent rules of the contest. As soon as the first kiss ended, another began, until Allegra and Mark were intertwined in each other's arms. Allegra reached for him as he buried his face against her neck. "That was really impressive," he whispered. "I've never seen anyone do that before."

She sat up, surprised. "What do you mean?" she asked. "But what did you do over there?" She pointed over at his fire.

He turned his head to glance at it and reached into his pocket, pulling out a book of matches. "I always use these," he said. "Try them some time. They're very useful."

"But—but what about your book?" she cried.

"My book? What book?"

"The one you wrote on camping. This one." She fumbled for her guidebook and handed it to him. "I found it on the boat this morning. See," she said, pointing to the title page, "*The Essentials of Camping*, by Mark Trackman."

Mark burst out laughing. "You've got to be kidding," he said. "Do you have any idea how old this book is? This Mark Trackman was my grandfather!"

She stared at him, dumbfounded. Turning back to the title page and checking the date, she saw that he was right. "You mean you—"

"I never started a fire with a stick in my life," he said. "No one does anymore."

"Well, I did," she said staunchly.

He laughed and patted her vigorously on the back. "So you did. You're really something, you know that?"

Allegra smiled and poured the soup into a pan, putting it on the fire to heat. Mark watched her hungrily, sniffing loudly as she uncovered the salad. "Don't drop any unsubtle hints," she said. "They just might work."

"Give in, Allegra," he said, running a finger down her back.

She didn't answer. He was so used to getting his way that she didn't want to give up so easily. She found a corkscrew and opened the wine, pouring some into a crystal wineglass.

"You even brought a real wineglass," Mark mumbled. "You thought of everything, didn't you?"

Allegra took a sip of wine and leaned back to savor the

taste. "Mmm," she purred. "This tastes wonderful out here in the open air."

"Are you really going to drink that all by yourself?"

She gave him a sidelong glance. "Are you going to give me that recipe for Michel's trout mousse?"

Mark threw back his head and laughed delightedly. "Touché. Okay," he agreed, digging in his pocket and producing the desired slip of paper. "You win." Allegra took the recipe and slipped it into her pack. "You know," he said more quietly, "I was going to give you that recipe when the contest was over."

Allegra said nothing, but she reached into her pack and produced another glass. Without a word, she filled it with wine and handed it to him. "Here you are," she said. "One recipe for one glass of wine."

They clinked glasses and drank, enjoying the blissfully fresh air and the solitude of the forest night for a few moments. Then Allegra unwrapped the trout mousse and picked up a fork. Mark also picked up a fork, but Allegra quickly grabbed his wrist. "Not so fast," she said. "What else do you have to trade? That trout mousse does not come cheap."

Mark eyed her shrewdly, now fully aware of her game plan. "You're serious, aren't you?" he asked grimly.

She said nothing, merely taking a taste of the mousse and relishing it with an audible sigh of satisfaction. "Luscious," she pronounced, gliding her tongue around the outside of her mouth. "Simply marvelous."

Mark watched her performance with growing apprehension. "This is ridiculous," he burst out. "You can't starve me into submission!"

"Why not?" she asked with a little shrug. She dished some chicken and salad onto her plate and checked the soup which was bubbling gently.

Mark peered into the pot's contents and groaned. "I can't stand this," he announced. "You have to feed me."

"Do I?" she asked, taking a taste of the soup with one finger. Its creamy smoothness was like velvet, and she cleaned her finger with a gentle smack. "Mmmm," she said. "Heaven."

"I'll give you a ride back on the boat tomorrow in exchange," he offered.

"I can always catch a bus." Allegra shrugged. "Or hop a ride with someone else."

He frowned. "How about a weekend trip to any beach on the northeast coast? You can pick your weekend."

"I already have reservations for a week on Nantucket," she countered. "No deal."

"A Caribbean cruise?"

"Not interested."

"Well, how about a trip across the ocean?" he shouted, losing patience. "That's worth a piece of chicken and a bowl of soup, don't you think?"

Allegra was unmoved. "Sorry, not interested." She offered no further comment as she poured soup into a china bowl.

"All right," he said with an air of finality. "I'm sick of this game." He reached out to take a piece of chicken and Allegra swiftly countered by lifting the plate and aiming it toward the fire. "You're crazy!" he exclaimed, throwing his hands up. "You'd really do that, wouldn't you?"

"I'd rather starve."

He nodded several times and slapped his hands on his knees. "Okay, I get it. I know what you want." She looked up. "You want the third floor of the club, don't you?"

Her eyes sparked with interest. "Then we have a deal?"

Mark didn't answer, but he leaned over and left a searing, quickly arousing kiss on her mouth. Once again she felt her resolve slipping away, and she closed her eyes as the intensity of his touch stole into her blood. Mark's hand clasped the back of her head as his tongue sought the inside of her mouth. The night began to swirl around her as she willingly lost her sense of time and place. His mouth lifted from hers, and he spoke in a stinging whisper. "No deal, Allegra," he said. Allegra fell back to earth. Her eyes blinked open in astonishment as he stood up stubbornly. "I'd rather starve." He marched back to his own campsite without a backward glance.

Chapter Eight

Allegra learned quickly that guilt is an interesting emotion with a set of politics all its own.

As the sky turned from dark blue to black, she felt much less triumphant than she had expected. Night burst into full bloom as she sat in front of her fire with too much food. The moon rose high over the mountains, and a glittering rash of stars appeared. Having never seen so many stars all at once in the sky, Allegra realized what a citified person she really was. A flock of wild ducks flew by overhead, leaving eerie echoes of their wild calls, and she savored the beauty of the night alone as she sipped the excellent wine.

Mark was no longer visible across the clearing, but she could see the beacon of his campfire. The silence between them was louder than any argument could have been. Despite the array of food in front of her, she had the curious feeling that he was the victor and she was stuck with the spoils of a battle she had never wanted to fight.

She took a long, slow breath. There was only one way out of this nonsense. "Mark?" she called, trying to sound neutral.

There was a pause. "What?" he called back at last.

"Would you like to help dish out the soup?"

At first he was stunned. "Soup?" he repeated.

"Well, you don't think I'd let you starve, do you?"

There was another ominous pause, but evidently Mark was not going to let pride conquer hunger. He got up and strolled over to her campsite, staring down at the feast she had spread out on a blanket. "No strings?" he asked warily.

"No strings. Come on." She gestured hospitably, and he believed her, plopping down to survey the bounty of food. Not only had Allegra brought a gourmet banquet, she had also packed beautiful pieces of china and silver, linen napkins, crystal goblets carefully wrapped in towels, and even two candles and candlesticks. Mark smiled as she lit them.

"You thought of everything, didn't you?" He began to laugh. "And you carried all of this up here by yourself!" The thought struck him as very funny, and he chuckled as Allegra dished soup into his bowl. "You probably made hiking history!"

Allegra wasn't laughing, but she was rather proud of what she had done. "I hope you agree now that it was all worth it," she said. "If it weren't for me, we'd be starving right now."

"Very true," he agreed, taking a sip of wine.

"You are camping with the president of the Mangia Society, and this is how she camps out. With real food—not powdered junk." Allegra served all of the food and examined it appreciatively. "Go ahead," she said and nodded. "Don't be shy. *Bon appétit*."

Mark sampled the soup and he looked up in surprise. "This is delicious," he exclaimed. "What's in it?"

She smiled. "Oh, the usual. Plus some secret ingredients of my own. Fennel, marjoram, and a little garlic, in case you're wondering."

The soup disappeared quickly, its creamy smoothness

warming their bodies and calming their spirits. The forest night seemed very vibrant now, silent and yet filled with the hint of life all around them. A summer wind blew down from the treetops, stirring the fire and wafting through Allegra's hair. They were so hungry that they said little, but a new and peaceful rapport had sprung up between them, and they were completely comfortable with the silence. The smoky, sophisticated taste of the chicken was offset by the tangy mushroom and pea pod salad and the earthy flavor of the stuffed potatoes that Allegra had warmed directly in the embers of the fire. Mark kept shaking his head, awed by the feast.

"I really can't believe this," he said for the third time. "You have no idea what you've done here. When did you cook all of this stuff?"

"This morning, while we were heading upstream," she said with a shrug. "It was no big deal. I can do a much more elaborate spread than this. Of course, all I had was—"

"More elaborate? Are you kidding?" He sat up with a sudden inspiration. "How would you like to do an article for my magazine?"

Allegra blinked in surprise. "An article? On what?"

"On outdoor cooking. The gourmet backpacker. You could include recipes, cooking tips—whatever you like."

Allegra thought for a moment. "That's a great idea," she said. "But I think I'll use it in my own magazine. I've got a newsletter, remember?"

Mark said nothing, but his eyes were fired with a sudden new energy as if he were thinking very hard about something. He ate the rest of the meal and Allegra finally brewed the Jamaican coffee she had brought and presented dessert. As Mark washed off the dishes with Perrier, Allegra poured the coffee. They sat next to each other on a log, listening to the persistent wind that sometimes played tricks on their ears. Mark's arm went around her and she leaned against him as they gazed up at the sparkling sky. The leaves rustled gently, and now and again the sound of a little creature scurrying by made Allegra jump. Mark reassured her that there was nothing to worry about, but she was not so sure.

"What about the bears?" she asked worriedly. "Shouldn't we have a weapon or something?"

"Don't worry," he said, snuggling closer. "Here, drink your coffee." She sipped the rich brew and handed him a tart. He devoured it with relish, marveling at the combination of the piquant fruit and the buttery crust. "Aren't you going to eat yours?" he asked, licking the last of the glaze from his fingers. She shook her head nervously. "Look," he said. "If there are bears nearby, all you have to do is make a loud noise and they'll run away. There's a whole chapter on bears in that book of yours." He picked it up and handed it to her.

Allegra flipped through the pages and found a picture of a huge grizzly bear towering over a tiny tent. Its claws were extended menacingly, reaching for the tent, and Allegra winced. "Oh, no!" she exclaimed, her panic rising. "That thing is a monster. Is this supposed to comfort me?"

"It's a grizzly," Mark said coolly. "There isn't a grizzly within hundreds of miles."

Allegra was not convinced. "Well, why do they call this place Bear Mountain?" she insisted.

Mark started to laugh. "It's probably just a name," he said, brushing her fear aside. "Don't be so nervous. We're two hours from New York City, for heaven's sake. This isn't Alaska, you know."

"Well, just the same," Allegra said, looking around in the night air for signs of anything moving, "I don't like the idea of anything bigger than myself hanging around my campsite." A new thought struck her and she looked up at Mark. "What about all this food?" she asked. "You said the smell alone would attract all kinds of animals. It says in the book that—"

"I know what it says," Mark interrupted her. "I read it when I was ten. Now stop getting yourself all worked up about nothing. I've never been attacked at a campsite in my life, and I've been in real jungles with animals a lot more dangerous."

"You were never lost before, either," she couldn't resist pointing out. She reached over and picked up a long, heavy stick, hitting it against the ground a few times to test its strength. "This will stop any bear," she said between clenched teeth, trying to muster up some courage. Mark burst out laughing.

"What's so funny?" she asked.

"You," he said between chuckles. "I can just see you trying to hit a bear with that thing. You look like the Cowardly Lion." She grimaced as his laughter continued, and he gave her a playful punch in the ribs. Suddenly he stopped short, his eyes sparkling in the firelight.

"What?" she asked at once. "What is it?"

"One of the items on the list just flew by."

"Flew by?" She looked around wildly. "Where?"

"There it is again," Mark said quietly, pointing into the blackness. He stood up lightly and moved into the shadows, his feet barely making a sound on the soft ground. He stood as motionless as an Indian, and for one eerie moment Allegra couldn't see him at all.

"Mark," she called uncertainly. "What is it?"

"Come and look," he said calmly, breaking the spell.

"There are a bunch of them over here. Hundreds, and they're beautiful."

Her curiosity overtook her, and she ran to his side. In front of him, flying relentlessly back and forth among the trees, were hundreds of fireflies. As each one lit up for a split second an ethereal glow of blinking lights made the night shimmer with magic. They stood transfixed for several minutes as nature displayed one of her most enchanting spectacles. Allegra didn't know how long they watched until one tiny fly suddenly lit up close to Mark's face. Very carefully, he reached out and slowly enveloped the little creature in his hand. Its light shone through his fingers as he captured it.

"Let me see it," Allegra breathed as he opened his hand a fraction. The firefly's strange glow lit up his palm as if his hand was possessed by magic.

"There's a mosquito net in my pack," he whispered.

Allegra scurried over and rummaged through his pack until she found the net. She handed it to him and watched as he gently placed the firefly inside.

"Let me get one now," she said. She walked forward toward the trees, where hundreds of fireflies were dashing about. It was easy to reach up and snare one. Allegra's catch went in the net with Mark's and they watched as the two tiny lights flickered on and off.

Mark's arms went around her suddenly and he looked down at her with a passion that surprised and thrilled her. "I've never met anyone quite like you," he said in wonder. His face was open and vulnerable, and beyond it she could see the moon and the stars and the whole forest aglow with fireflies. "Most people go into the wilderness and learn to adapt to nature," he said. "But you . . ." He shook his head and smiled. "You manage to make the forest adapt to you."

Allegra couldn't answer. She was mesmerized by the beauty of the night, by the wonders that lay hidden in the bounty of the earth, and most of all by the heart-stopping look in his eyes.

"You made me adapt to you as well," he mused. "I never thought I would ever feel this way about anyone"

"What way?" she dared to ask.

Mark looked as if he was about to reveal a part of him that no one had ever seen before. His eyes shone with a peculiar brightness that told Allegra he had been bottling up something very important for a very long time. She wisely refrained from pressing him any further. Perhaps he wasn't ready to articulate his feelings yet. Perhaps he wasn't even quite sure what they were.

She let her head fall back and drew his head down to her, kissing him gently and slowly. He responded gladly, his heartbeat jumping against her breasts as he took her into his strong arms. They kissed for what seemed like eternity in the middle of the forest. Allegra felt not only a sweet fire rising within her, but a sense of oneness and peace with the earth all around her. She and Mark were a part of nature's mystery, celebrating the sensations of life to their fullest. Mark's face, seared with passion, aroused her even more. His hair had fallen carelessly onto his forehead, and his eyes were narrowed with the fever of desire. He took her hand firmly and led her to the tent. They crawled inside, their faces shining in anticipation. Allegra started to reach for the buttons on her shirt, but Mark's hand stopped her.

"Let me," he whispered hoarsely.

She sat motionless as his hand moved slowly down the column of buttons, opening each one with a deliberate pause that was charged with electricity. When all of the buttons had been undone, he ran a finger down the center of her torso, letting it pass between her breasts. His hand slipped inside, gently covering one soft breast, squeezing it with just the slightest bit of pressure. Allegra wanted to tear off the shirt and offer him all of her sweetness, but she didn't move, letting him tease and arouse her with maddening slowness. His hand continued to play with her breast, savoring its heavy fullness, and all at once it darted to her nipple, which was already taut and awaiting his touch. He flicked a finger across it carelessly, and Allegra gasped. Pleased at her reaction, he continued to flick one finger back and forth, until she leaned forward, her breast on fire for him. His hand opened the flap of her shirt, finally exposing her breast, and the sight of it brought a flame to his eyes. He bent down and took the pink tip into his mouth, nibbling and caressing it with his tongue. Allegra fell back as Mark's strong body moved over her. His hand drew the other flap of her shirt aside and found her other breast quickly, holding it and arousing it before traveling down restlessly to the exquisite valley between her thighs. He stroked her body skillfully, bringing it easily to fiery heights, and her hips moved unconsciously beneath him in a frenzied dance of desire.

"Touch me," Mark whispered raggedly, and Allegra's eyes fluttered open. She tugged at his belt buckle and fumbled with his shirt buttons, struggling frantically in her passion to find the strong, lean body underneath. He sat up and helped her, shedding his clothes gracefully before lying back to let her work her magic for him. She began at his hard, flat stomach, tracing circles and drawing lines up the firm lines of his chest. Her mouth opened to tease the taut male nipples before gently flicking at the sturdy column of his throat. Her hand dropped to savor the strong, muscled cords of his thighs, reaching underneath to stroke the backs that had looked so lean under a pair of jeans. Mark moaned, and Allegra felt a little thrill. She loved pleasing him this way. Her hand moved to the sure source of his desire, when suddenly something cracked just outside the tent. She hesitated for a second and then ignored it, concentrating on the sensual pleasure at her hands. She stroked him with a slow, feather-light rhythm until his hips moved in the same dance that he had coaxed from her. The sound of a branch cracking made her sit up in alarm, even though Mark's hand was guiding hers back to his body. But Allegra heard the rustle of silver foil, and then the coffeepot that she had left near the fire fell with a sudden clatter. Allegra jumped, but Mark gave her a calm smile.

"Bears!" she said. "It's a bear, I know it."

"Shhh," Mark reassured her, but Allegra looked around stealthily, her concentration shattered. "It's only chipmunks," he said, fondling her breast. "We didn't put the food away and now they're having a feast. If it was a bear, you'd know it, believe me. You'd hear very heavy breathing and a low growl." He pulled her down next to him and pinned her underneath, growling in imitation of a bear. Allegra giggled, and he inserted a strong leg between her soft thighs. Her arms went back around his neck, but the next instant, she heard a loud bang that almost made her jump through the roof of the tent.

"This sounds awfully suspicious to me," she said, groping around for a flashlight. "I think we should investigate."

Mark fell back with a broad gesture. "Go ahead," he said. "But all you'll find is a bunch of chipmunks having an evening picnic." He laced his hands behind his head, making his chest muscles ripple, and she hesitated. "Don't be long," he added in such a seductive voice that she was tempted to forget the exploration. Another loud noise made up her mind.

She poked her head out of the tent very quietly, and heard something moving near the blanket. Carefully aiming her flashlight, the pot ready in her hand, she peered into the night. If there really was a bear, she decided she would rather know about it now. Suddenly a loud bang came from the direction of the fire, nearly scaring her out of her wits. In one swift motion, she smashed the pot down on a nearby rock and flicked on the flashlight. She screamed wildly in an effort to scare off whatever was out there, barely aware of Mark's laughter as she continued her tirade.

"Aaagh!" she screamed, banging the pot madly. "Get lost, bear! Go on, beat it!"

There was no further sound, and at last her voice died away, out of breath. Mark's laughter pealed merrily behind her as he took the flashlight from her hand. Sweeping the beam over the camping area, he searched calmly until he found the culprits, shining the light on their tiny faces.

"There you are," he said, following the paths of two furry chipmunks who were rushing away with potato skins in their mouths. "There's your ferocious bear."

Allegra let out a shaky sigh and turned to look at him. His face was still wreathed in mirth, but mercifully he was not making fun of her. She sank back into his arms, suddenly very grateful that he was there.

"Thank you," she said, managing a weak laugh.

"For what?"

"For not pointing out what a fool I've been."

He rocked her in his arms for several minutes as they listened to the wind and the hurried patter of their nocturnal visitors. The night was still and yet it was filled with life. Allegra closed her eyes against Mark's chest and thought to herself that this night was enchanted. Anything seemed possible. It was a midsummer night's dream.

"Mark . . ."

"Mmmm?"

"Where were we before we were so rudely interrupted?"

He lifted her chin and kissed her, letting his tongue part her lips and seek the warmth inside. He tasted of the clear, fresh night, and she felt safe and protected in the shelter of his arms.

Her hands fell to the trim lines of his waist and held on to the compact hips that shifted under her touch. She felt the latent power there, knowing that soon those masculine hips would be conducting a wild, primitive dance between them. Mark's hands roamed restlessly over the soft skin of her back, igniting her senses. They moved down to her rounded bottom, playing with the fullness and reaching around to touch her satiny thighs.

"You feel like a flower," he whispered. "A soft, fresh flower just ripe for the picking."

Allegra fell back and took him with her, her hands delighting in the silken skin that covered his body. Her breasts crushed against his chest, making the nipples tighten as they grazed his firmness.

"Every time I touch you like this," he said raggedly, "I want you so much it drives me insane." Allegra tried to nod, but her breath was caught in a gasp as he hungrily took a firm nipple into his mouth and nibbled it with lusty pleasure. He lifted his head and looked into her eyes. "Tell me you want me," he said.

"Oh, Mark . . . you know I do," she cried.

"Tell me."

"I want you. Please . . ." Her eyes beseeched him to

continue his slow, tormenting exploration of her body, and she watched through half-veiled eyes as his tawny head began a sensuous journey down her willing form, leaving fire wherever he touched her. He gathered her round, full breasts into both hands and feasted on their peaks with rotating flicks of his tongue. Allegra was lost in a sea of pleasure that was so intense she thought she might actually topple over the pinnacle from his caress alone. But Mark had more in store for her. He continued his journey, moving down to sample the round, sensitive flesh of her belly and parting her legs to feel the impossible softness of her inner thighs. Allegra's toes curled and her hips arched as she shuddered deliciously under his spell. He was so unhurried, so maddeningly deliberate. His tongue sought the sweet flow of her body, tasting it with tiny, butterfly strokes that sent her into a whirlpool of passion. Allegra was lost in a timeless eternity of pleasure. Never had she felt so utterly alive, every nerve and cell tingling and singing with awareness. Never had she felt so in tune with another human being who could give her this much sensual joy.

She tugged frantically at his sandy hair and he shifted his body so that she was able to reach the strong proof of his desire. She touched it and teased it with greedy abandon, reaching underneath to draw erotic patterns on the tight male buttocks.

Mark groaned and sat up, his arms clasped around the curve of her waist. He pulled her on top of him, letting her breasts fall onto his chest, and then he lay back on the blanket. Allegra straddled him and sat up straight, leaning over only to ease him inside of her. He filled her with a wondrous sense of power, as if he grew magically to a larger-than-life size once he had entered the sweet warmth of her body. She remained still for a long

moment, relishing the sense of completion. Mark's eyes
were wide open, and they moved over her pronounced
curves with naked enjoyment. His strong hands grasped
her hips and lifted them. He moved her body up and
down for a few moments, until she was overcome with
passion. Mark lay still then and watched her, letting her
take her pleasure from him as she would. She became a
wild, free spirit, charged with a savage grace, a forest
creature caught in the fundamental union of nature. She
had never felt so natural and so free, and her pleasure was
deep and earthy, as if it had sprung from the earth itself.
Mark's hands strayed to her shoulders, her breasts, her
hips, heightening the overwhelming flashes of sensual
need that were rising within her like a swelling tidal
wave.

At last her passion grew so intense that she fell forward, her hair partially falling across his face. Deftly
holding on to her hips, he gave a sudden push and they
turned over, still deeply joined together. Allegra moaned
in utter abandon, instantly wrapping her legs around his
hips. He was the leader now, moving with strong, hungry thrusts that created an erotic rhythm. She felt that
she could not get close enough to him, could not take in
all that had happened between them. And she needed
desperately to do that, to cross the final barrier into his
heart. The searing sensuality became laced with an
urgent longing, one so strong that it brought sudden tears
to her eyes. She clung to him feverishly, receiving him as
a dry well receives spring water.

His strong arms moved under her back, gripping her to
him so that every inch of their bodies were interlocked.
They passed through an invisible gate and found a new
rhythm, one that was slower than the driving rhythm
they had just left, but one that was nevertheless tinged

with deep desire. Allegra shut her eyes tight and saw the colors of the earth flash before her eyelids. Mark drove into her even more deeply than before, and suddenly they ceased to be two bodies struggling in passion and became one magnificent, timeless force that had no beginning and no end. The sensations enveloping them were one and the same, and together they were hurled into a whirlwind of response, together they clutched and triumphed in its peak, and together they cried out their release into the forest night.

Several long, lovely moments passed before Allegra realized that they were floating on a cloud headed for earth. The cloud meandered its way down until she was able to open her eyes and remember where she was. Mark was still firmly on top of her and her legs were still wrapped around him. Slowly she let them slide down, and he shifted his weight so that their bodies were finally parted. She sighed a little at her reluctance to let him go, even then. As long as he had remained inside of her, the magic had lingered.

Mark lay next to her and held her snugly against him, slowly stroking the soft curves of her body. "That was exquisite," he said simply, knowing that he was confirming rather than suggesting.

"Yes." Her answer was equally direct. The communication between them was on a high plane that transcended mundane reality. "Mark . . ." She stopped, faltering.

"Yes?"

"I've never felt this way about anyone before. Never."

He sighed tremulously. "Neither have I."

She paused, searching for the right words. "Have you ever been in love?" she asked boldly.

"No," he admitted honestly.

"You haven't?"

He shook his head. "Not really. I've had my share of impetuous flings . . ." His hand found hers and held it. "But nothing like this."

She sighed then, whispering the tremulous sound of a woman on the brink of love. It barely seemed possible that Mark Trackman, her landlord and the editor of the magazine she had so recently scorned, was falling in love—with her. And even more incredibly, she was falling in love with him.

Now that they had stopped being at odds, her feelings for him were mushrooming into new dimensions that she could hardly understand or control. She realized dimly that all of their banter had been the underside of what was happening between them now; it had been their way of reaching out and touching each other. There had never been any real hostility in their fighting and Allegra would be sorry to ever let it go completely because it had sharpened her wits and had forced her to respect him. More than once she had caught herself smirking privately at one of his well-aimed jests. She turned her head and smiled as she recalled the turgid prose of *Trailblazer*. It wasn't badly written, actually. It reflected the romanticism and boundless enthusiasm of a small boy with big dreams. "You're really a little boy at heart, aren't you?" she asked suddenly.

To her profound surprise, Mark nodded seriously. "No one has ever known it but me. And now you." A long look passed between them, a look that spoke volumes. "How can you know me so well?" he asked.

"I don't know," she whispered, as awed as he was. "But I'm so very glad that I do." She shifted her body so that one thigh was thrown over him. "Little boys can be very hard to tame."

He laughed softly and slipped a hand between her legs, burrowing it into the softness. "Don't try to tame me," he warned. "Just remember that no matter what little boy demons are lurking inside of me, I still have the appetites of a grown man."

Allegra thought about that, a slow smile curving the corners of her mouth. The combination was absolutely delicious.

Chapter Nine

❦

Just before dawn Allegra awoke to the sound of Mark's deep, low breathing. At first it didn't bother her and she tried to go back to sleep, but the sound grew louder, turning into snoring, and she reluctantly opened her eyes.

"Hey," she said sleepily, rubbing her bare leg against his.

He turned in the sleeping bag, uttering a long, low "Mmmm."

"Mark," she said half coherently. "You're snoring."

"I don't snore," he mumbled indignantly.

"But you were—" Allegra stopped and gasped in mid-sentence as she heard a loud snort.

"Now what?" Mark moaned.

"Shhhh!" Allegra commanded. "I think I hear something!"

Sure enough, a snoring sound could be heard again, and Allegra knew with a sinking heart that it wasn't Mark. She listened with growing fear as she heard food being kicked around outside the tent. Suddenly a pot fell to the ground, making her bolt upright.

"It's a bear," she said in a loud whisper. "Get up!" She pushed at Mark a few times, but he didn't budge. "Hey," she repeated. "It's a bear. This time I'm certain."

Mark snuggled down in the sleeping bag, his hand resting lazily on her warm backside. She watched in dismay as he went right back to sleep.

Outside, she detected unpleasant sounds of loud, boisterous eating. "Mark?" she whispered, giving him a well-placed nudge. "Will a bear ever attack a tent?"

"It might," he mumbled sleepily. "If he thinks there's food inside."

Allegra froze. Outside someone or something was making its way over to the garbage. She could hear the plastic bag being ripped into shreds.

Mark opened one eye and looked at her. "Allegra," he said patiently. "How many times do I have to tell you? Those noises are being made by chipmunks. We didn't tie up our food or put it above the ground. It's like sending out an engraved invitation." He smiled drowsily. "Maybe the chipmunks are having a scavenger hunt too."

She was about to smile, but the loud noise of a backpack tumbling over changed her mind. "Can a chipmunk push over a backpack?" she asked skeptically.

Mark shot up and listened intently. Allegra handed him the flashlight wordlessly and watched as his smile faded and he grew sharply alert. Something that was definitely bigger than a bread box was feasting only a few feet away.

"I don't like the sound of that breathing," Allegra whispered.

They listened and detected a heavy whistling sound, but it soon ended. Mark relaxed after a moment and his patient smile returned. "It's the wind in the trees," he said decisively, trying to pull her back down.

"Are you sure?" She frowned as he kissed her neck and took her earlobe into his mouth. It sent a tingle through her blood, but he could still sense her apprehension. "Look," he said, "I've been on hundreds of camping trips in places a lot less secure than this. And it always turned out that the things that went bump in the night were chipmunks."

She said nothing, stubbornly silent, and he threw back the covers impatiently. "All right, all right," he muttered. "I'll go take a look if that's what you want." He grabbed a pair of jeans and climbed into them hastily. Allegra knew he was annoyed, but she didn't care. She was positive she was right.

"Be careful," she said fearfully.

Mark shrugged her off and picked up the flashlight. Slowly unzipping the front of the tent, he climbed out and disappeared into the darkness.

"Be careful," Allegra said again, listening nervously for the sound of his footsteps. She quickly pulled one of Mark's sweat shirts over her head and pulled on a pair of jeans. She peeked through the flap and saw the flashlight beam whipping back and forth as he searched the area. Then several ominous seconds went by during which there was no sound at all, only the beam of light shining into the forest.

Suddenly Mark's voice broke the stillness. "What a mess!" he said. "There's food all over the place. Those chipmunks are unbelievable. I've never seen them do this much damage." He waited a little longer, but nothing happened. Just as Allegra was starting to regret her insistence, Mark froze.

"Wait a minute," he said tensely. "What's this?"

"What's what?" she asked anxiously. She scrambled out of the tent. "What is it?" she called. "Mark! . . . Mark?"

"Get back in the tent," he said tersely. "There are footprints all over the ground." He aimed the flashlight at the earth, and she made out a zigzag pattern of oversized paw prints. Before she had time to think, there was a low growl only a few feet away.

Mark's flashlight shot up instantly to cast full light on a huge black bear that was rummaging near the food. In its paw was the remainder of Allegra's apricot tart. As soon as she saw it, she let out a scream and reached automatically for the nearest object. In a second she was banging the pot against a rock, while Mark shone the light steadily in the bear's face.

The animal did a fast about-face, holding up a paw to keep the light out of its eyes. It ran off into the forest like a scared jackrabbit and vanished. Allegra continued making a racket and was still going at it full force when Mark walked over to her and put his hand on her shoulder.

"You can stop that noise now," he said calmly. "The bear's gone."

She stopped immediately and dropped the pot. It fell to the ground with a clatter and Mark led her back inside the tent. He took her in his arms with a little laugh. "You continue to surprise me," he said, stroking her back soothingly. "You looked like an Amazon warrior out there, going into battle."

She managed a weak smile. "I was just angry," she said wonderingly. "I really wasn't afraid."

"Angry?"

"Yes," she explained. "All I could see was that apricot tart. I was saving it for lunch tomorrow. That bear had a lot of nerve."

Mark laughed again and pulled her down, burying his face in her tousled hair. "You are incorrigible," he said.

"There's the original turnoff point from yesterday,"

Mark announced. They had backtracked through the maze of trees, trying to find the white markers, and now they were back at the place where they had both left the main trail. Allegra took her pack off and sat on a large rock and looked around. It was the same rock that Sabrina had been sitting on the day before when she had directed Allegra into the woods.

"Did you notice something, Mark?" she asked, frowning. "The white markers all looked faded today, as if someone had tried to erase them all."

He looked up and nodded thoughtfully. "Water-based paint," he agreed. "Definitely suspicious."

"This is right where Sabrina was sitting yesterday," Allegra continued. "She was the one who pointed me in the wrong direction."

Mark's eyes lit up. "You too? That's how I got lost!" He shook his head in amazement. "She must have a terrible sense of direction."

"No, she doesn't." Allegra sighed. "Although her sense of humor is definitely open to question at this moment." He was puzzled. "Oh, Mark, don't you see? Sabrina didn't make a mistake." She stood up and examined the rock. Sure enough, a white arrow was there, a clear, indelible one that had been hidden by her legs. It was not pointing in the direction from which they had just come. It was pointing straight up the mountain.

"We've been tricked!" Mark exclaimed, rubbing his head in consternation.

"Not tricked. Set up." Allegra smiled ruefully and plunked down again on the rock. "By my mischievous friend, Sabrina the Incurable Matchmaker."

Mark whistled. "I think you're right. But I also think there are even more people involved than her. Think for a second. Who came up with the idea of having a scavenger hunt in the first place?"

She looked at him. "Wendell."

Mark said nothing. He picked up her pack and handed it to her. "Come on," he said. "Let's go." He turned in the direction of the mountain peak.

"Go?" she said. "But why? Why do we have to reach the top now? Probably everyone is gone by now. Whatever is up there is long gone."

"I just want to see what's going on here. Besides, we made it this far. I'd like to say I hiked to the top of Bear Mountain and back. And the view must be terrific." He held out a hand and she took it.

To their everlasting surprise, they found that the summit was only three-quarters of a mile from where they stood. They had almost been there when Sabrina had misguided them. Allegra walked easily, relieved of much of the heavy burden she had been carrying the day before, and in no time at all they were standing on a long ledge that overlooked the entire valley and the park below. Allegra peered down and saw the parking lot all the way at the bottom. Beyond that, Mark's yacht lay peacefully anchored in the Hudson River.

Then her eyes whipped back to the parking lot. "There are no cars!" she cried. "Everybody is gone!"

Mark was looking all around the ledge. "Well, that's no surprise. I don't see anyone else up here." He gave a short laugh. "We've been had, Allegra."

"Well, what should we do now?"

"I don't know about you, but I want to look for that final item Wendell said would be up here."

"But Mark." She walked over to him and looked up into his eyes. "It will be long gone. Someone must have taken it last night."

He shook his head. "I'm not so sure. I have a sneaky suspicion that there is more to this whole setup than meets the eye." He took off his pack and let it drop down. After a moment Allegra did the same, following him across the ledge. They walked carefully for a few minutes until they found another small, scruffy trail that led upward for an additional forty feet. They stopped and looked at each other, knowing instinctively that this was it.

Allegra frowned. "Zeebo would never have climbed this. I know him."

"I don't think he climbed it," Mark said. "But I do think that someone else did. Come on." He began to climb the steep ascent, extending his hand down to help her up. Together they slowly made their way up, clawing and struggling to find footholds in the rocky surface, and after several laborious minutes Mark hauled her up to a high plateau.

Allegra sank down, breathing hard. "Whew!" she said. "I'm glad I didn't have to climb *that* with a pack on!" She looked around, instantly refreshed by the clear, clean air and the spectacular vistas that stretched in all directions. Allegra felt she was on top of the whole world at that moment. No matter what happened after this, at least she would be able to say that she had stood at the very pinnacle of a mountain that she had climbed by herself. But Mark wasn't looking at the view. He was looking down. His sudden burst of laughter startled her out of her reverie.

"Look at this!" he said, pointing at the ground. Allegra looked and saw a large, prominent arrow that had been carefully drawn into the earth. "And this!" She followed his gaze and saw another arrow a few feet away. They lifted their eyes and opened their mouths in astonishment as they realized that a whole path of huge, unmistakable arrows had been carved into the ground, obviously leading to the final destination of the hunt.

They walked slowly, holding hands and saying nothing, neither wanting to mar the heady feeling of suspense. Arrow after arrow guided them until they found themselves in a small meadow filled with wild flowers. The arrows had stopped, but Mark pointed suddenly to a small mound in the middle of the grass. Allegra broke free and ran over to it, stopping abruptly when she saw what was there.

Sitting by itself on top of the mound was a lone can of white paint, mostly empty. Stuck inside the paint can was a used paintbrush.

"Well," Allegra said dubiously, "I think we have snared the final item."

Mark draped an arm around her and grinned. "It looks like they left it here especially for us."

"Lucky us," she said dryly, picking up the can. The brush was stuck fast to the paint, making it look like a pop-art sculpture. "I guess we should get going."

Mark laughed and pointed down into the trees. "Look," he said. "See anything familiar?"

Allegra stared but could see nothing except the long expanse of trees. Then her eyes focused on a little clearing with a dead campfire in it. "That's our campsite!" she exclaimed, turning to face him.

"That's right." He nodded. "It was only about a hundred yards away. We were extremely close to the top all along."

Allegra laughed weakly and sighed with relief. "Well, at least we weren't as lost as we thought."

He took her in his arms and kissed her. "I wouldn't have missed a moment of it for the world."

Chapter Ten

At nine-thirty that evening, the outside of the Gotham Men's Club looked more like a convention for junk collectors than the stalwart fortress it was supposed to be. The members of the Mangia Society were milling around, swapping stories of their adventures over the past few days. The street was filled with all sorts of strange items, and passersby cast strange glances as they looked at all the paraphernalia. Allegra had taken a cab down from her apartment on the West Side, and as the car pulled up in front of the club, she gasped incredulously at the odd sight.

"My God!" she said. "Look at all that stuff!"

Her eyes fell on the huge bear she and her friends had gotten the day before. Next to it was a street sign that said DON'T EVEN *THINK* OF PARKING HERE. Other items were piled in a crazy heap that spilled over into the street, making it difficult for the cab to get close to the curb. Allegra paid the driver quickly as horns blared impatiently behind her. When she emerged, a huge cheer went up from the women's team. Veronica and Sabrina rushed over to greet her.

"Well, how did it go?" Sabrina asked coyly.

"You two," Allegra said, feigning indignance, "are the

sneakiest, the most conniving—especially you, Sabrina. Here," she added, handing Sabrina the can of paint. "This is yours, no doubt."

Sabrina took it with a guilty expression, but another hand reached over and took it away from her. Wendell stood there with the can of paint in his hand and smiled. "Mine," he said smoothly. "In my younger days I pulled the same prank on my fellow club members. Old habits die hard." He gave them another smile and walked to the doors of the club. Sabrina looked at his retreating form in amazement. "He really is something," she said, shaking her head. "And I thought I was crafty."

Opening the club doors, Wendell gestured for them all to come in. "Are you sure?" Allegra asked. "Won't we be disturbing your members?"

Wendell laughed dryly. "Don't be silly," he insisted. "There's no one here after six o'clock. Come in, and bring all your findings with you!"

They all trooped inside, subdued into respectful silence at the faded grandeur of the lobby. Colin studied the old paintings and photos of former explorers in their glory and let out a low whistle. "I'm impressed," he said.

The others echoed his reaction. As they walked through the rooms, they felt as if they were invading a private home. Wendell led them to the lounge with its grand old wing chairs and Victorian draperies, and the stuffy room came alive with the low muffled voices of so many people. No one spoke above a hushed tone, but the buzz of conversation filled the empty room. Wendell stood in the middle of the room and waited as a few stragglers dragged in the last of the larger items. Veronica was hauling the bear inside, placing it right next to the trophy head of a moose.

"This place is something," Dan said to his wife in greeting.

"It has a venerable charm," she agreed, letting the bear collapse on the rug.

"Would you all kindly move back while we begin our inventory?" Wendell said. He had taken a seat on an old settee near the fireplace, and he leaned forward on his cane. When they had all quieted down, he looked up expectantly. "Shall we begin?"

"Where's Mark?" Colin whispered fiercely to Dan. "He's got most of our stuff in his car."

Allegra shifted uncomfortably, wondering the same thing. It was a quarter to ten. He had only fifteen minutes more.

Everyone pressed forward eagerly and found a place. Some people sat on the chairs and sofas; those who didn't sat on the floor. Mark still hadn't appeared, and Wendell looked around, noticing the absence. "Where is Mr. Trackman?" he asked, looking directly at Allegra.

She had no answer, and he checked his watch. "Well, we're a little early. But since everyone else is here, let us begin." He picked up a copy of the list. "The first item is the recipe for the trout mousse. Did anyone get that?"

"I have it," Allegra said uncertainly. She felt distinctly guilty producing it, but its appearance caused a startled reaction from everyone else in the room.

"Where did you get it?" Veronica asked excitedly.

"Score one for our side!" Sabrina called out merrily, snatching the piece of paper out of Allegra's hand. She ran over to Wendell and handed it to him.

"Wait a minute," Colin called out. "We have that item too. Mark has it." Dan nodded vigorously in agreement, and Wendell frowned.

"We will come back to this item at the end," he decided. "If and when Mr. Trackman appears," he added, making them fall back, subdued. "Now, the next item is the street sign."

Both teams had procured this item, and Wendell checked off scores for both sides with a little chuckle.

"The playbill!" he called out. Sabrina produced that item proudly, and Colin groaned.

"Just don't forget to return it tomorrow," he reminded her. "Or we're out a thousand bucks."

"Where the hell is Trackman?" Dan whispered fiercely. "It's ten o'clock!"

"There he is," Allegra said brightly, pointing to the door. Everyone turned and followed her gaze. Mark was standing in the doorway carrying a fantastic conglomeration of junk, all of it stuck haplessly together.

Mark ignored the reaction he was creating and appealed to Wendell. "Excuse me," he said calmly. "But does the gallon of glue have to be wet?"

Everyone burst out laughing as Mark made his way through the crowd and deposited the collection of items in front of Wendell. "I'm afraid I have to deliver these all together," he said. "There's no way to get them apart."

"Fine, fine," Wendell said, unperturbed. "That's the kind of ingenuity I like to see." Mark smiled and moved back into the crowd, looking for Allegra and finding her seated next to a large potted palm. To her embarrassment and delight, he sat down next to her and put a strong arm around her, drawing her close. She flushed and looked down at the floor, but she knew that Sabrina and Veronica were looking at her like two grandmothers who had made a perfect match.

Wendell continued going down the list, checking off

items one by one as they were delivered. The score remained very close, and they waited with mounting anticipation for the final results. By eleven-fifteen, Wendell was approaching the end of the list, and still there was no front runner. It was clearly going to be a race to the finish.

"And the very last item," Wendell announced dramatically, "are the fireflies. Will both sides bring their findings, please?" Allegra and Mark looked at each other and stood up. Mark was carrying the mosquito net and they walked forward together.

"Here you are," he said to Wendell. "Two fireflies— one from each side."

Everyone stared as the two tiny lights flickered silently in the shadow of the mantel, and Wendell checked off the item on the list. "Well," he announced, looking up. "It appears that the ladies have won. By one point."

Sabrina jumped up and cheered lustily, and the rest of the women followed suit, hugging each other and congratulating themselves on a fine victory. But Colin held up his hand and called for silence, finally lifting Sabrina onto his lap and holding her firmly.

"Wait a minute, everyone!" he called out in a commanding voice. "There is one more score to settle!"

Wendell stood up and quieted the room, his erect posture and pleasantly dry voice subduing them once again. Gradually they all settled down and listened as Colin stepped forward to address them.

"I believe it's a tie," he said, squelching the enthusiasm of the women.

Sabrina frowned. "What do you mean?" she asked darkly.

"I mean," he continued, "that we have one more item to produce. Mark?" He looked around and found Mark still standing in front of the fireplace next to Allegra and Wendell. "Would you turn in the recipe for the trout mousse, please?"

There was a moment of utter silence. Then Mark answered simply, "I don't have it."

Colin's face fell. "What do you mean, you don't have it? I thought you—" He gestured insistently, willing them all to believe him. "We had it yesterday," he said to Wendell. "I know we did."

"Well, where is it now?" Wendell asked.

Mark gestured toward Allegra. "I gave it to her," he said.

This was greeted by another silence, this one bewildered and confused. "But—but why on earth did you do that?" Dan asked, voicing all of their thoughts.

"It was a trade," Mark explained.

They all stared at him, fascinated. "Go on," Wendell encouraged him.

"I had no food last night," Mark continued pointedly, looking at Sabrina. "And as I believe you all know, Allegra and I were lost. She had brought up an entirely prepared feast, and I traded her the recipe in exchange for a meal. It's that simple."

This information was absorbed by the group as Wendell chuckled to himself. "Well, well," he mused, "in that case, I suppose it is a tie."

"No, it's not!" Allegra announced suddenly, making everyone look up. "The trade wasn't fair. I tricked him into it. The men's team has the recipe, and they have won the scavenger hunt!"

Her remark caused an uproar that was immediately interrupted by Mark. "That's not true!" he insisted. "It was perfectly fair. The women have won."

The group broke into loud arguments, with members

from both teams taking both sides. Veronica thought the men's team had won, and Sabrina thought it should be a tie. Colin agreed that the women had won, and he and Veronica tried to convince Dan that the whole contest could still come to a fair and logical conclusion. Several minutes went by during which everyone had an opinion and no one had a solution. Finally Wendell called for attention, and they all stopped to listen, grateful for an objective viewpoint.

"I am the judge of this contest," he announced. "And I shall decide the outcome. Does everyone agree?" They all nodded eagerly, waiting for his verdict.

"I believe," he continued, "that we should take a vote. The winner shall be decided by a democratic majority." He looked around. "Now, how many vote for the women's team?" Several hands were raised as members from both sides voted. Wendell quickly counted the hands and jotted the number on a pad. "And how many vote for the men's team?" Allegra raised her hand and looked at Mark. Her face was flooded with emotions, some of them so new that she could not conceal them at all. She couldn't believe that he had wanted to hand her the victory. It was so magnanimous of him, so gallant, so sportsmanlike. Wendell counted the hands, but she was hardly aware of the tabulation. As far as she was concerned, Mark had won a greater victory than any mere contest could provide. He had won her respect, her admiration, and her love. All of these feelings warred in her face as she looked at him, and his eyes melted with a new intensity as he read her heart.

"I'm afraid we still don't have a winner," Wendell announced suddenly. "Too many of you have abstained. The only fair thing to do is to declare a tie."

The room broke into pandemonium as hands were clasped and backs were slapped. The tie was much sweeter and more rewarding than the victory they had all striven so hard to attain. Mark looked down at Allegra and took both of her hands in his.

"I think we've all been had," he said gently. "Wendell is an old fox."

"What do you mean?" she asked.

"I mean that I think he knew all along what would happen. Not just between you and me, but between all of us. Don't you see?" he pressed earnestly. "The compromise is greater than all of us. It's something we had to learn to appreciate, something we had to work for. We were so busy competing that it never occurred to us that there was a better way."

Allegra's eyes crinkled as her old spirit returned in full force. "Oh, can it, Trackman," she said. "Don't start preaching at me. Let's get down to business here. Do I get the third floor of the club or not?"

Mark laughed uproariously and threw his arms around her, drawing her close. "You are delicious!" he exclaimed. "I love you."

The full effect of this disclosure was smoothly interrupted by Wendell, who stepped up to them with a smug little grin. "Actually, my boy," he said dryly, "the issue of the third floor is not your concern. As a matter of fact, it has already been decided." Mark looked up with one eyebrow raised. "Look around you," Wendell said, opening his arms in a broad gesture. "Look at all these fresh young faces. Wake up, Mark. This old club is being reborn." He turned to Allegra. "You may use the third floor for entertaining any time after six o'clock. Agreed?"

She clasped his hand in a hearty handshake. "Agreed." She nodded happily.

"Good. Any problems?" he shot at Mark.

Mark's face changed slowly as a huge grin spread across his features. "No problems," he said at last. Wendell sauntered away, and Mark chuckled softly. "Leave it to him to get that settled," he said. "And I'm very glad too."

"Are you, Mark?" she asked quietly.

He nodded. "Of course I am." She said nothing. "Oh, come on, Russo," he said impatiently, cupping her face in his hands. "You know what I mean. I'm not too good at mushy declarations, but I do know one thing. You and I belong together, and I'm not going to let you go. And once I make up my mind, I don't take no for an answer."

Allegra smiled radiantly, her happiness glowing in her eyes. "For once," she said, "I'm not going to give you an argument."

Then she was lost as he wrapped his arms around her and kissed her, sealing their truce in front of Sabrina, Veronica, Wendell, and the entire Mangia Society.

"Look!" Sabrina said, pointing at them triumphantly. "I knew it all along! Before long we'll be hearing wedding bells, you'll see."

Mark and Allegra looked up at these words and Allegra pointed a finger at her friend. "Sabrina Melendey," she warned, "I know you've already got something up your sleeve."

Sabrina looked wounded. "Why, whatever gave you an idea like that?" she asked innocently. She looked at Veronica and smiled. The two of them walked away together, whispering feverishly as Allegra groaned.

"Don't worry about them," Mark said, drawing her

close again. "If whatever they're planning works as well as their last scheme, you and I should have nothing to worry about."

Allegra couldn't have agreed more.

RAPTURE ROMANCE

*Provocative and sensual,
passionate and tender—
the magic and mystery of love
in all its many guises*

NEW TITLES AVAILABLE NOW

(0451)

#93 ☐ **TOUCH THE SUN by JoAnn Robb.** When aerial photographer Alinda Jamison agreed to work for Drew Fletcher, she knew the job came with risks even more dangerous than flying. One tender kiss from this patient, handsome man took her to heights of ecstasy she'd never dreamed possible. But love brought fear, too . . . Could she survive a crash into heartbreak or was this love strong enough to soar forever . . . ?(130065—$1.95)*

#94 ☐ **A DREAM TO SHARE by Deborah Benet.** Handsome Olympic champion Kell King wanted beautiful Orin O'Malley for his partner—to share his dream of becoming the world's best in professional pairs skating. Their fire on ice swept Orin into a dizzying spin of desire. But would falling in love be enough to melt a heart turned cold with a secret—and a fear—that could destroy her career . . . and her chance with Kell? (130073—$1.95)

#95 ☐ **HIDDEN FIRES by Diana Morgan.** Gourmet food expert Allegra Russo was both enraged and enraptured by ruggedly handsome Mark Trackman, a confirmed male chauvinist. A business deal brought them into confrontation, and while his attitude toward working women infuriated her, his sweet kisses sparked a passion she couldn't deny. Allegra wanted Mark and his love, yet she was unsure if their professional differences would keep her from winning his heart. . . .(130081—$1.95)*

#96 ☐ **BROKEN PROMISES by Jillian Roth.** Alison Mitchell was a genius with computers . . . but a failure with men. Badly scarred from a disastrous marriage, she buried herself in work, until Curt Ross swept into her life. The most sensuous man she'd ever met, his fiery kisses were irresistible. But even as the bond between them seemed to grow stronger, Ali wondered if she dare trust any man again—even Curt. . . . (130103—$1.95)*

To order, please use coupon on last page.

RAPTURE ROMANCE

*Provocative and sensual,
passionate and tender—
the magic and mystery of love
in all its many guises*

COMING NEXT MONTH

LOVE AND LILACS by Kathryn Kent. Gourmet chef aboard an exclusive private yacht, McLain Rutherford was thinking only of business—and not of confident First Mate Coby Hunter. Yet the soft ocean breeze and Coby's moonlight kisses proved irresistible. But then McLain found out that Coby was an ambitious restaurateur and she had to decide if he really loved her, or if he was just trying to use her—and her recipes—to make his own business a success. . . .

PASSION'S HUE by Anna McClure. Art journalist Daria Barrow was determined to get an exclusive interview with prickly artist Michael Kramer. But the aloof painter was tender, too, she discovered when she became his model—then his lover in an exciting, sensual affair. Yet Michael's "love them, paint them, leave them" reputation worried Daria. When her portrait was finished, would their love be over, too . . . ?

ARIEL'S SONG by Barbara Blacktree. Karen Watts was swept away by sensual Ariel Singer's sweet, searing kisses—and by a deep desire that only his exquisite lovemaking could satisfy. Yet for Arial, love was a game, lovely fun but never played for long . . . and for Karen, anything less than forever would never be enough . . . .

WOLFE'S PREY by JoAnn Robb. At last, a romance from *his* point of view! Pursuing an art smuggler, undercover agent Jason Wolfe wasn't prepared for beautiful gallery owner Dana McBride. Warm, kind, sensual, she made him realize everything he'd been missing in life. Jason would've given anything to let her know how he felt . . . but he knew she'd only be hurt more when she discovered who he really was. This time Wolfe was caught in his own trap—and he wasn't even sure if he wanted to get free . . . .

RAPTURE ROMANCE

*Provocative and sensual,
passionate and tender—
the magic and mystery of love
in all its many guises*

Titles of Special Interest from
RAPTURE ROMANCE

**Buy them at your local
bookstore or use coupon
on next page for ordering.**

RAPTURE ROMANCE

*Provocative and sensual,
passionate and tender—
the magic and mystery of love
in all its many guises*

RAPTURE ROMANCE

*Provocative and sensual,
passionate and tender—
the magic and mystery of love
in all its many guises*

RAPTURE ROMANCE

Provocative and sensual, passionate and tender— the magic and mystery of love in all its many guises

---

**Buy them at your local
bookstore or use coupon
on next page for ordering.**